Shedding

Narrow

Fields

A. M. McClain

DEDICATION

For my family.

CONTENTS

ACKNOWLEDGMENTS

My thanks go out to T. M., E. G., L. H., W. A., G. W., G. G. M., C. A., and many others; also, to M. D., J. C., for the driving sounds. I would also like to thank *you* for showing me that there is more in this world than what is directly in front of me, and for reading this, my first work. Thank you!

I.

The young child, who not long ago turned nine years old, sat in the living room of the tiny two-bedroom house. He sat on the floor with his back resting against the leg of the couch, staring intensely at the flashing lights and nearly chaotic array of noises leaping from the screen. It was late; about 11:30 p.m. He could feel the time. He let out a heavy yawn, then rubbed his eyes.

"Martin!" yelled the voice of an older woman.

The child pretended not to hear.

"Martin!" she yelled as she walked into the room. She made her way to him, leaned down and grabbed him by his left ear.

"Ack!" Martin yelped in pain as she gave a slight twist to his ear.

"Didn't you hear me calling you, boy?" she asked.

Martin, with a small tear welled in his eye, sat shaking his head pitifully.

"Let's go. It's time to get ready for bed."

"Yes, Gramma," he sobbed.

Martin followed his grandmother to the bathroom where he brushed his teeth and washed his face, then changed into his night clothes. Once finished, he went into his room.

"Say your prayers!" Gramma yelled from the living room.

Martin mimicked her by mouthing her exact words, laughing, and then dancing a raunchy solo number. Suddenly, he heard his grandmother's footsteps coming toward his room. He immediately jumped to the side of his bed, fell to his knees, and began to pretend a prayer.

"Ah-men," he whispered as Gramma walked through the door.

Martin did not see it, but Gramma was holding in a chuckle as he finished his prayer. She knew all too well that he didn't speak one word to God. "Get in the bed," she commanded.

The young man jumped onto the mattress, pulled the single cover back and wiggled his way under it. Once under, Gramma tossed the blanket over him. Martin then squirmed his way into a comfortable position and, once he found it, Gramma tucked the covers under him, then gently smoothed the rest of the blanket over the unoccupied area of the bed with her hand.

After he was all tucked in, Martin lay still with his eyes closed as if he had already fallen asleep. Gramma remained next to him on his bed, studying his face, rediscovering all of the features the boy inherited from his mother. "Yep," she thought, "he has her pointed nose, her little ears, and those bushy eyebrows she spent half her life plucking out."

Suddenly, Martin opened his eyes. "Can you tell me a story about mamma?" he asked, as if he knew she was thinking about her only daughter, her only child.

"What do you want to hear, sweetie?"

"Can you tell me about... how... when she and my dad met?"

"I sure can, baby," she said with a smile. "Go ahead, close your eyes and listen," she began as she rested the palm of her right hand atop his forehead. "Your mama'," she continued, "was about thirteen when she met your father. She was so beautiful then; smart too. She had the biggest, brightest brown eyes. All the boys, and some *dirty* men, talked about those eyes of hers. They said they held two of the most precious diamonds in the world." Gramma talked as Martin lay quietly, eyes open. She had her head tilted up, eyes gazing dreamily at something on the ceiling. She continued, "She had the smoothest skin; never had a pimple in her life, and was the color of rich caramel.

"When she met your father, she was in middle-school. She had straight A's, and was takin' all the hard classes: Algebra, English, and Music. They met one night at the school dance. She went alone. He saw her from across the room. She didn't even see him coming, but he walked up to her and asked her to dance. She said no, but he kept asking. Finally, your mother gave up and told him that she'll dance with him, but during the *next* song. The last song ended, and he, quick as lightnin', was standing right next to her, his hand out waitin' for hers. She was shy and embarrassed; it was her first dance with a boy. She gave him her hand and he took it, then he led her to the dance floor. He pulled her close, but she resisted. Then the music played; it was 'I Wanna' Get Next to You' by Rose Royce.

"As the song played on, they danced closer and closer together. By the middle of the song, she let him pull her hips right up to his. She thought she heard him whisperin' along to the song, so she looked up to see if it was really him singin' or if it was her imagination. Well, she looked up and saw him singin' with a smile on his face. Then she moved up to look at his sleepy eyes, and when she got there she was caught. They stared at each other for a minute, then he whispered right in sync with the song, 'I wanna' get next to you'. Then, he leaned into her, and she leaned into him, and they kissed. Poor thing was hooked after that!" Gramma said, then looked down at Martin. He was fast asleep. She breathed a deep sigh then stood up.

As she raised herself from the bed, Gramma shook her head. "Poor thing," she thought as she gazed at the sleeping child. He had been asking her about his parents for years now; had always wanted to know how the two met. He had asked her for other stories, but this was the one he most enjoyed. Unfortunately, this story, the one he liked most, was a lie. At least, it was not what happened to *his* mother. The story Gramma told was hers; about how she met her first love. Though, the song was different.

The truth was, Gramma did not know how Martin's parents met. In fact, there were so many boys coming and going that she was never sure she had *ever* met his father. It was true that his mother was beautiful, indeed. She took heavily after Gramma. But she was not a scholar to the degree in which she was portrayed in the story. She actually had very poor grades and had skipped school quite often.

Gramma then reached her head down and kissed Martin gently on his forehead. The boy did not stir. She walked through the door and closed it, leaving just a crack of light shining in, and went to bed.

II.

It was the middle of the day, about one thirty. Young Marlene lay in bed napping, dreaming about the kitty she had when she was four years old. He was such a fluffy, white feline. She was sitting in her room which looked different, but she knew it was hers, gently petting him. She began to sing an improvised song to him: "Mr. Kitty, you are soft. Mr. Kitty, I love you so much!" Suddenly, she heard a low growling sound coming from behind her. She froze as she felt the hot breath molesting her neck. The monster let out another low growl, then a heavy "Bark!" in the girl's left ear. Marlene let out a yelp, then with her left hand covered her mouth and, with her right, pulled Mr. Kitty closer to herself, hiding him from the monster.

The beast then walked from behind her, revealing itself. It was a big, black as shadow she-devil dog whose eyes glowed blood red and had foam falling from its mouth. The mutt walked up to Marlene and put its snout into her face, then began sniffing. It smelled something; something it wanted. She let out another low growl, then another loud bark. Marlene raised both hands to cover her ears. Mr. Kitty ran from her and into an empty corner of the room; the beast ran close behind.

The dog and cat stood, face to face, in the corner, each growling in their respective tones. Marlene knew what was to come, so she closed her eyes as tightly as she could and held her hands over her ears just as firmly. She could hear it, though faintly; the dog began her attack. The kitten fought back as much as he could, but he stood no chance against the wretched she-beast.

When the noise stopped, Marlene opened her eyes, her hands still fixed over her ears. She looked in the corner. The dog was gone. All that was left was a bloody pile of kitty entrails sitting in a pool of thick, crimson liquid. Everything suddenly went black.

Instantly, Marlene woke up, her heart beating furiously. Tiny beads of cool sweat covered her face. She looked around and realized she was in her actual room. In the corner was a pile of dirty clothes; no blood or entrails. She breathed slowly and deliberately, and began to calm after she realized that it was all just a dream. She then pushed the covers off of herself then sat up on the edge of her bed, let out a yawn and rubbed her eyes. She scratched her head, stood up and walked to her bedroom door, turned the knob and opened it just a crack, and listened. There were no footsteps, was no commotion heard besides the distant sound of music playing on the television in the living room. She slowly pulled the door open, trying to keep it from creaking, and just enough so that only her tiny frame could slip through.

The hall was lit dimly by the sunlight which came in from the sliding glass door in the kitchen. It must have been the only light in the house. Marlene gently crept through the hall and into the living room. She could now clearly hear the raucous music videos playing on the television. She knew her father was there watching the girls dance, and could see his arm resting on the respective rest of the recliner, which sat directly in front of the television screen.

Marlene quietly walked up to the chair where the man's arm was resting, reached up and slowly dragged her fingers across her father's arm, from the elbow up to his wrist. He did not move; he knew she was there. She was not as quiet as she thought she was. The man pretended to sleep as she peeked up at his face and waited for a smile to appear. Still, he did not move. She then walked around and stood right in front of him and tickled his knees. Still, nothing. Marlene became flustered, frustrated even; she knew she could break him. She raised her right hand and began to reach for his naval. Suddenly, the man popped open his eyes, reached down with both hands and grabbed his daughter beneath her arms. He then let out a playful growl as he tossed Marlene in the air and very gently caught her. They both laughed as the man pulled her onto his lap.

"Daddy," she whispered. "You scared me."

"I'm sorry, baby girl," the man replied.

"Watcha' doin'?"

"Just watching T. V."

Marlene turned to see what he was watching. On the screen was a famous female pop star. She was singing a fast song; the child noticed how fast the singer's mouth was moving, and how strange it was that the woman kept her eyes glued hungrily to the camera. The singer sat lounging poolside in a white and gold bikini which barely covered her most personal areas. The scene suddenly changed, and the woman was standing with several other female dancers around her, all were moving their hips around frantically to the rhythm of the beat.

Marlene looked up at her father. His eyes were stuck to the screen. He then broke his trance and looked down at his daughter. He nodded his head toward the television. Marlene took his direction and focused back on the screen.

"She's beautiful," her father said dreamily after a moment's pause.

Marlene said nothing. Again she looked at her father and noticed a shiny, glazed look in the man's eyes as he stared at the starlet singing and shaking herself on the television. Marlene then turned back to the screen. The previous song ended, and the singer was gone, only to be replaced by another beautiful songstress who sang fast and moved her hips wildly.

Just then, as if summoned by way of magic, Marlene's mother appeared from behind the recliner.

"John!" she yelled at the man. "What have I told you about letting this child watch this trash?!"

Marlene's father rolled his eyes and let out an audible sigh. "It's not gonna' hurt the girl, Jackie," he calmly replied.

"You don't know that!" she screamed, then reached down and grabbed the remote control which lay on the headrest of the recliner. She lifted the device and pointed it at the television as if it were a futuristic weapon aimed right at the heart of her enemy.

"Get up, girl," the woman said to the child. "Go

wash up for dinner."

Without reply, Marlene reached up and gave her father a gentle peck on the cheek, climbed off of him, then sorrowfully marched back down the dark hall to the bathroom. As she went, she heard her mother yell something incoherently, then her father yelled louder a reply just as indecipherable.

"Why the *fuck* are you letting that girl watch this trash, these *whores* on this television?! Didn't I tell you I don't want her to grow up idolizing such ... *shit*?!" she said her curse words quietly, yet with emphasis.

"Babe, it's just a little T. V. She'll be fine. I'll be sure of it –"

"How can you be so sure?" she snapped. "You're not *fine*. You can't even get a job! You're telling *me* you'll make sure she'll be fine, when you *yourself* are a massive pile of ..."

"Say it!"

"Never mind."

"Say it, bitch!" he yelled.

"You're a pile of shit! You always have been and always will be! If it wasn't for Marlene, I would have left you years ago!"

John sat, red eyed and crimson cheeked, breathing heavily. He let out an intense roar, "Raaaaah!" which could be heard throughout the house.

Marlene, who had long finished washing up, stood in the hallway, having heard the final exchange between her parents. Suddenly, John stood up and, without looking at anyone, furiously walked to the front door, opened it, stepped out and closed it with a terrifying Slam! that shook the whole house. Marlene's mother, in a huff, quickly marched into the kitchen to finish preparing dinner. Marlene, the poor child, stood alone in the dark hallway. Tears were streaming down her face.

III.

"Okay, class," began Ms. Rodinsky, a third – grade teacher at Marshall Elementary School. The entire class raised their little heads and eyes toward her. "Okay," she continued, "at this time, we are going to get into groups, then we are going to work on our arithmetic worksheet."

The class let out an audible, collective sigh.

"Now, I don't want to hear that." Ms. Rodinsky said, addressing the entire class. "Okay, I decided to mix up the class this time. Listen for your names. You will be placed in groups of two. Here we go! James and Richard. Antonio and Vanessa. Okay, let's see. Martin and Marlene. Hector L. and Daria."

Just then, a student in the back of the class raised his hand. "Yes?" the teacher asked the boy.

"You said Hector? Which one? Hector L. or Hector H.?"

"It was Hector, hmmm, Hector L." replied Ms. Rodinsky.

"Oh. Thank you Ms. R.," said the boy.

"I said Hector L., didn't I? I was pretty sure that's what I said."

A big smile appeared on the child's face. "Oh. I think you did." he said as his cheeks turned red, embarrassed by his mistake.

As the teacher continued calling out the rest of the groups, Martin and Marlene both stood up and had attempted to move to one another's desks. Once Martin reached the girl's table, he realized she was not there and began to look around the room for her. As his eyes shifted to his own desk, he saw her standing there with her hand on her hip, waiting for the boy to return. Martin tried to give her a stern look, as if to say "You come back over here!" but the girl never looked at him. Frustrated, Martin slowly walked back to his seat.

As Martin retook his original chair, Marlene, still not looking directly at him, slammed her math worksheet and pencil on the desk across from Martin's. She then pulled the tiny plastic chair from beneath and sat quickly, heavily on it.

"How do you do this?" Martin began. There was no reply. "Hey, how..." he continued but, upon looking up at the girl, he realized she had quietly started her work, and was about halfway finished with the front page. Martin sighed. He began to feel alienated, all alone and lost. He was not good at math, and the person who was supposed to work with him did not even acknowledge his presence.

"Hey!" Martin said with a raised voice. Marlene unflinchingly continued her work, so he slammed his open hand on the desk at which she sat. She slowly raised her head and gave Martin a hard stare.

"What?" she asked, sternly.

"We need to work together."

"No, we don't."

"Ms. R. said we need to work in groups!" Martin whined.

"I'm almost done. I'll let you see my paper when I'm finished," she said, then threw her eyes right back down onto the worksheet.

Martin was upset, but glad she was going to share her work with him. Math had always been difficult for him. Every time he looked at the numbers, they would start to change. They would begin to dance around the page, confusing him. Lately, he has not so much as tried to make an attempt at working the problems, as his mind would shift from math to music, and he let it. He would daydream about being one of the guys he had seen in music videos on television. He imagined himself wearing brand new clothes, shiny sunglasses, and resting on boats in the middle of the ocean. He hated that life for a child meant that he could not have anything he wanted. If he was like them, he could have it all. Nobody would tell him that he couldn't. Nobody could tell him what to do. He would call the shots. He would decide whether or not to do math worksheets!

"Martin," a distant voice called.

He thought he heard somebody calling him, but it was faint. He was lost in his fabulous dreams.

"Martin!" cried Ms. Rodinsky.

Martin came back into the classroom. He looked up and saw his teacher staring down at him, then looked at Marlene who was sitting back in her chair, arms crossed in a dignified way, and playfully shaking her head with an heir of haughtiness.

"Martin, are you alright?" Ms. Rodinsky asked

softly.

"Yeah ... uh ... I mean, yes Ms. R." Martin replied.

"How much of your math have you completed?"

Martin looked down at his paper. It was exposed for all to see, so there was no use in his telling something other than the truth.

"Marlene is finished, Martin. Go sit next to her and she will help you," she said this addressing both Marlene and Martin, and she said it with an authoritative tone, yet kept a caring smile on her face.

"Yes, Ms R." Martin said, then sat for a moment as if waiting for his teacher to walk away. Ms. Rodinsky stayed beside his desk, smiling and nodding, waiting for Martin to move first. He stood up, defeated, and slowly shuffled to the desk next to Marlene.

"You're gonna' get in trouble," Marlene sneered at him.

"Na-ah!" Martin replied.

Once Marlene went back to work, Martin tried to look over at her paper, but she had her arms blocking his view. She noticed him trying to see over her arms, so she covered the entire paper with her body. While her head was down, she smiled and tried desperately to keep herself from laughing at the poor boy.

"I thought you were gonna' let me see it," Martin said.

Marlene turned her head toward him then stuck out her tongue.

Martin gasped. "I'm telling teacher."

"Okay, okay," she said as she lifted herself from atop the worksheet.

Martin looked at her paper and feverishly began to

copy exactly every number, word, and mark of any kind the girl had put down. At this point, Marlene was finished playing with him. She let him copy his paper for about thirty seconds, then she pulled her paper away and out of sight.

"You can't do that!" Martin cried.

"Well, you shouldn't be so stupid," she casually said.

Martin became angry. His cheeks reddened and he began to breathe heavily.

"Don't... call... me that," he huffed.

"I'll call you whatever I want. I'll call you stupid, and I'll call you a bastard."

A look of confusion overcame the boy. "A what? What's that?"

"That means you don't have any parents. My mom told me," she replied mockingly.

At that remark Martin became enraged. "At least my parents never beat each other up."

"My parents don't beat each other!"

"Uh – huh. I live right across the street from you guys, and I saw them that time the police came and took your daddy away. Your mamma was outside screaming and blood was on her head." Martin smiled as he finished. "I got her," he thought to himself.

Suddenly, Marlene let out a ferocious scream. She stood up and jumped on Martin. She grabbed him by his curly hair and began pulling as hard as she could. Martin tried to stop her. He stood up, but she still had a tight grip on him. She gave a hard yank, and they both fell over. Martin scrambled and was able to break free from her grasp. He then jumped on her as she lay on the floor. Before Martin could throw a punch, Marlene reached up and dug her finger nails into his face and neck. Ms. Rodinsky quickly ran to the two children then grabbed Martin around his waist and pulled him off of the girl. As she held him, Martin began to cry, to weep, and all of the children watched, astonished. Martin looked around. Marlene was calm, dusting herself off, and the other children simply gazed at him. Some pointed and laughed.

IV.

It all goes so fast. When one looks back, he only sees points of memory, instances of gross pain or pleasure that dug so deep as to leave an everlasting imprint on the mind. When one looks forward, he only sees that which is believed to be impending. The anticipation builds awaiting these future points in time, yet they inevitably come and, just like the rest, they go.

For Martin and Marlene, years have passed. They are no longer the young individuals traversing the narrow fields of middle – childhood. They are no longer concerned with colors inside of the lines. Their minds are no longer preoccupied with worries regarding whether or not "Johnny" meant it when he said he didn't want to be friends anymore. They had shed that prepubescent mindset. They are now both thirteen years old, adolescents, and are entering into a world that stands in stark contrast to that which they have just left behind. They are growing, yet are not grown. They are children who are struggling with the demands of minds which are fighting their way into adulthood.

It was the end of spring, and it was hot outside. School

had just ended for the year, and summer would be fast approaching. At this time, in Los Angeles, it did not matter if the calendar counted this time of year as spring, the weather was sweltering and it will remain to do so until around late October to early November.

Marlene, now thirteen years old, was sitting on her bed after having awaken late in the afternoon. She pushed her hair up and rubbed the sleepiness from her eyes. Then she picked up her cell phone. No alerts, no messages. She scrolled quickly through her applications and tapped on the camera button. She lifted the phone up, pointed the screen downward at her face, then stared hard at the image shown on the face of the screen. She reached her hand up to her eye and removed a hair which rested near the corner, on top of her cheekbone. She flicked the hair off of her fingers, then focused back on the camera.

Young Marlene pulled some of her hair down to messily cover her forehead. She then squinted her eyes to make it look as if she had just, that second, woken up from an intensely deep sleep. With her thumb, she pressed a button on the side of the device and a photo was taken; the sound of a shutter accompanied the action. She looked carefully at the photo, analyzed each section then decided it was no good. She rearranged her face into the sleepy configuration she had worn previously, then carefully pressed the button again. "No," she thought. She pulled some of her hair she put on her forehead back atop her head. She reset, then took another photo. She was satisfied.

Marlene then sent the photo to her boyfriend Andrew, who she met just before school ended. She sat staring at her phone, waiting for him to reply, but nothing came. She waited a few more seconds, nearly an entire minute, but still nothing. She sighed, then stood up and moved to the full length mirror in the corner of the room, just behind the door. She stood there, staring at the scene which the mirror reflected. She noticed how much she had changed over the past year. She was slightly taller, for sure. But, without taking into account her increased length, she noticed more that she had gained weight. She had been on a diet for the last couple of months, and really pushed it when Andrew, one day, playfully pinched her hip and said, "Wow, you have a lot of skin here." She got upset. Not so much that he uttered those insensitive words, but because it was something she had been working on, yet it still remained.

Marlene turned to her side and lifted up her shirt, exposing her waist and abdomen. She noticed a slight protrusion just below her belly button. She took a deep breath, sucking in her stomach. She stared for a second and thought, "That's what it *should* look like." Then she turned to face the mirror. She noticed her curves; the way her body waved as she guided her eyes from her neck, over her breasts and back down into the troughs of her waist, finally back up over her widening hips. "I'm getting *so fat,*" she thought. Yet she weighed only ninety pounds, and was already five feet, three inches tall.

The young girl sighed at the sight of herself, and produced a pout that nearly reached the soft white carpet below. Her stomach, suddenly, let out a low growl. She looked down and shushed it, "Sshh!" She felt the pangs of hunger, for she had nothing substantial to eat since the afternoon of the previous day. Still, she decided not to eat. Instead, she picked up her phone, tucked it behind the elastic waistband of her pink pajama pants, and headed for the bathroom to shower.

Later, after bathing, Marlene sat in the living room, on the comfortable brown recliner, watching music videos. Her mother was at work and her father was still asleep in the other room. It was then two-thirty and Andrew still had not replied to her photo message.

"Marlie!" her father suddenly called out from the bedroom.

Marlene rolled her eyes and smiled at hearing him call her "Marlie". She then stood up and walked down the hall and to the door of the man's bedroom. She turned the knob and pushed the door open just an inch. She put her face to the opening and with one eye, peeked inside. Her father was still lying in bed, his eyes closed. He was on top of the covers with just a pair of boxer shorts on. She looked at the bottoms of his feet. They were clean and white, with no sign of callous. She moved her eye up his legs, which had a fair amount of coarse hair covering them. Then she surveyed his abdomen which pointed skyward as the man was laying on his back; the same hairs as seen on his legs trailed down the center. She noticed his belly had become rather large. Her gaze rose to his chest, which lay bare and hairless in the open air. Finally, she reached his face and was startled when she saw a pair of dark brown eyes staring back at her.

"Marlene," the man said, as he knew she was at the door.

The girl slowly pushed the door open and walked inside. She gently glided up to the side of the bed where her father was laying. He watched her carefully as she made each step. He noticed the way her hips shifted from side to side as she walked. Marlene, forgetting how much she had grown, suddenly jumped on the man. He let out a heavy, painful groan, then grabbed his daughter around her waist and gently pushed her onto the bed next to him. His face displayed a countenance of confusion as the girl lay next to him laughing at his pain.

"What are you doing, sweetie?" he asked her.

"I was just watching T. V.," she replied.

He then looked deeply into her eyes quietly for a moment as if lost in thought. She looked back. He then reached out and brushed the hair from her forehead, then followed with a light brush of her cheek with the back of his hand. She smiled at him. He smiled back.

"You're getting so big," he said, still smiling.

"I am?" she said in a whisper.

John nodded his head. He reached his hand back out and rested it on her shoulder. "You're almost a woman," he said.

Marlene could feel the blood rush to her cheeks. She felt nervous about her father talking to her in that manner. Not sure exactly how to respond, the girl kept still and quiet.

"You've grown so beautifully," he said as he moved his hand down her side, resting it now on her waist. Marlene swallowed audibly. Her father continued to smile, yet she lost hers. She felt like jumping up and running away, he was making her so very nervous.

"Shhh," he said as he moved his hand over her belly. He began moving it lower and lower. Marlene closed her eyes, then everything disappeared. There was no sound, no movement, and no feeling. The world around her had just vanished.

Marlene awoke with a gasp. Violently, she sat up as if trying to push an enormous weight off of her. She looked around and saw that she was still in her father's room. She was still on the bed, and was the only one there. She looked down. The bed had been made. Everything in the room was neat and clean. She could feel her heart beating, and her breathing was grotesquely labored. She reached her hand up to her face to wipe away the sweat she could feel rolling down her cheeks; but she could not *feel* anything. There was no perception of the sensation of her hand touching her face. Upon looking, on her fingertips was water, yet she could not feel it.

The girl then stood up next to the bed. A sudden numbness overtook her, and a dizziness overcame her head. She felt as though she was going to fall over, but she kept her balance. She began to walk toward the door. As she moved, she could not feel her feet on the carpet; she could not feel herself taking steps. She only felt something of an inner pressure in the very depths of her body. She looked down at her feet. They were there, and everything looked normal. Then she looked up to see that she was suddenly standing in front of the bedroom door. She reached out and grabbed hold of the brass knob. She made to turn it, but it would not move. It was as if it was locked from the outside. She turned and twisted and wrenched it harder and harder, but nothing. She began to cry then sank to the floor in despair. She rolled herself into a fetal position, her arms wrapped around her knees which she brought up to her chest, then cried herself to sleep.

"Beep, beep, beep, beep," a distant sound was heard.

"Beep, beep, beep, beep," a moment later came the sound again.

"My phone," Marlene thought to herself. She opened her eyes and quickly realized she was not in her own room, nor was she on the floor. She was on her father's bed. She looked around the room and found she was the only one there. The bed was a mess, as was the rest of the room. "Beep, beep, beep, beep." cried her phone again. She stood up and began looking for it, desperately following the sound of the alarm. "Beep, beep, beep, beep." It went off again. Marlene heard it coming from the other side of the bed. She got up and walked around. "Beep, beep, beep, beep." Her eyes immediately flew to the place where the sound was coming from. She looked down and saw a pair of boxer shorts, the ones her father had on earlier. She reached her foot out and kicked the shorts, revealing her noisy phone.

She reached down and picked up the device, hoping for some word from Andrew. She pressed a round button on the front of the phone and the screen lit up. Immediately, she saw an image that resembled a battery. It was blinking red and had an exclamation point in the middle of it. "Beep, beep, beep, beep!" it rang louder and displayed the words, "Low Battery."

Marlene was suddenly overcome with emptiness, sadness and despair. She felt tears trying to force themselves from her eyes, but she fought hard to keep them in. She looked up and ran her eyes around a room she felt she did not want to be in. She slowly walked to the door which was wide open. As she moved, she could feel an odd slipperiness between her upper thighs. She began to walk faster as an intense fear started creeping over her. She walked straight into her room, closed the door and locked it behind her. Then, without a moment's thought, she jumped into bed and began letting out the tears which she could no longer suppress.

V.

Martin, who was no longer the small, pitiful child he once was, and who was becoming more like a man every day, was in his room getting ready to leave the house to spend time with some friends from school. On his bed lay a pair of ironed denim pants; black. A roll of black socks, ankle highs, quite short, were resting atop the jeans. Under his bed, just below the hanging legs of the pants, were a pair of black tennis shoes; immaculately clean, as if brand new. Martin was standing in front of an ironing board, gently taking out the wrinkles of a blue, black, and white flannel shirt. He stood, wearing just a tank top and a pair of athletically styled boxer-brief underwear.

In the corner of the room was a writing desk, atop which sat a couple of old photos, a computer monitor and a pair of speakers. Just below the desk were the actual computer and a small black box which held another speaker; a bass speaker. As he ironed, Martin listened to music. He was listening to one of his hip – hop heroes, a rapper who went by the name of Little Big G-sta. When his favorite song came on, Martin walked to the computer and turned a small knob on one of the little speakers atop the desk. The volume of the music increased dramatically. After a few seconds past with just drum, some bass, and a bit of wavy electronic keyboard music playing, Little Big G-sta began, and Martin sang along:

> "I smacked that foo, fuh tawkin' shit!
> "I smacked that foo, den ah' smacked his bitch!"

Just then Gramma ran to Martin's door and began wrenching on the locked knob.

"Boy, turn that down!" screamed Gramma.

Martin could not hear a word, and continued ironing the wrinkles out of his shirt, and ironing creases in. The song continued to play:

> "Then I grabbed the girl, and I rubbed her stuff,
> "Then I told her to scream when she had enough!"

Gramma began slamming her fists into the door, intent on either getting his attention or breaking down the door, whichever happened to occur first.

Martin finished his ironing job. He gently lifted the shirt by the shoulder seams, slowly walked to the side of his bed, and laid it over his pants forming a human pattern that simply needed a body to jump in, filling it.

The song came to an end and Martin began to hear the pounding of Gramma's fists on the door. He then very coolly and calmly turned toward the door, and walked to it slowly, allowing the old woman a few more heavy pounds of her fists. The next song on the record began to play as he reached the door. He let out a sigh, then turned back toward the computer and walked over, just as slowly as was his shuffle *to* the door, to turn the music down. As the knocking continued, he walked back to the door, unlocked it, and opened it with a crooked grin on his face.

"Boy!" Gramma started. "I've told you too many times not to play that stuff so loud in here! And I *especially* told you about playin' that *trash* in *my house*, didn't I?!"

Martin tried desperately to keep up his aloof manner, but Gramma always had a way with her words that made him feel like the two year old child he was when she took him in after his mother left. After her quick interrogation, he simply lowered his head and eyes and nodded pitifully.

"Boy, if I hear it again, I'm sendin' you right back to your mamma, you hear me?" she said, looking down at the wretched child. She took a quick look around the room and saw how clean it was. She saw how neatly and meticulously everything was arranged; how straight and well hung the poster of Little Big G-sta was on his wall. She then looked at his bed, which was well made and tight. She noticed the clothing which rested stop the mattress covers.

"You goin' somewhere, sweetie?" she asked the boy gently.

"Yes, Gramma," he said trying not to sound sarcastic, as he knew she was sure to tell him otherwise, that he was not going anywhere.

"Where you headed to?"

"I was just gonna' go see some friends. We were gonna' go to the park. The one next to the high school."

Gramma looked at him sternly, as if at a chessboard, trying to figure out her opponent's next moves. "Okay, sweetie. You all be safe out there, okay?"

Martin looked up at his Grandmother, a smile stretched across his face. He crept up to her and wrapped his unusually long arms around the woman. "Thanks Gramma. We will." he said to her. She planted a kiss atop his head; she was still about four inches taller than the boy, but she knew that was going quickly to change.

"Okay, baby. Gramma's gonna' go do some readin' in her room. Don't let me hear that music again," she reminded him. Martin just nodded and smiled.

After Gramma left, Martin quietly shut the door, walked to his bed and began putting on his clothes. As he pulled on his pants, tied his shoes, and carefully wrapped his shirt around himself, he daydreamed about the day he would leave that house. He imagined himself in a recording studio, like the ones he had seen on television, working with rappers like Little Big G-sta. He would be in the booth with his mouth up to the mic, and Little Big G-sta would be at the control board with champagne and beautiful women. Every now and then Little Big G-sta would raise his head after a bobbing session, look Martin in the eyes, and give him a big thumbs up.

Those were Martin's dreams for the future. He was not worried about going to college. He was not all too concerned about high school either. He was determined to be rich through rapping in just a few years. But, for now, he had to go meet his friends. So, after he dressed and dreamed, he stood up and left the house.

It was hot outside, Martin noticed as he walked along toward the park where he was to meet his friends. He looked around with squinted eyes. Reflections of the sun were coming at him from just about every surface. He looked ahead toward the horizon and saw only waves of heat wiggling about, bending light waves with ferocity. He lowered his eyes and continued his march.

As he reached the corner at the end of the block where he lived, he saw a small group of birds sitting in the shade beneath a tree that was not small, nor was it large. It had just enough foliage on it to accommodate the three or four birds seeking a couple degrees of relief from the heat.

"Guh!" Martin blurted as he walked past the tree. "Guh?" he thought to himself. "Where did that come from? It's too hot today."

After another ten minutes of walking in the intense heat, Martin reached the park. It was not a large park. It had fields of grass and trees, two small baseball diamonds used mostly by little league players during early Spring, and one full basketball court which, on the rims, had metal chain linked hoops that let out a "Chang!" every time the ball went through it.

Near the basketball court stood a small structure made of wood. It looked like a tiny house, yet it held the park's major electrical controls and meters. Martin knew this because one night he and the same group of friends broke open the lock with a pair of bolt cutter his friend Joey brought from home. They all went in using the light of their cell phones to see, hoping to find something incredible. All they found were switches, dials and knobs, and a few black widow spiders. The outside of the very same control room was now the place where he and his friends spent their time.

Martin, in a hurry to get out of the direct blasts of sunlight and into the cool shade provided by the side of the electricity hut, quickly made his way to the hang out spot. As he approached, he saw his friends standing there. With them were a couple of young people Martin had never seen before. He looked closely to try to make out who was all there. He saw Joey with the same red baseball cap worn backward as he always wore atop his head. He saw Michael with his rounded spectacles on his face, which he constantly pushed up the bridge of his nose as he talked. There was Terrence in his long basketball shorts. Then there were two others. He looked harder, hoping their faces would look familiar, but, as he got closer, he realized that they were strangers and that they were a few years older than the rest of the boys.

"Hey! Martin!" yelled Joey as Martin neared.

Martin said nothing until he was standing with the rest of the gang. "What's goin' on, guys?" Martin asked.

"Hey." "W'sup?" "How's it goin', Martin?" came various greeting from the group of youngsters.

Martin looked up at the two unfamiliar faces and gave them a quick head nod. They both responded with the same gesture. One of them gave Martin a hard stare after his greeting as if sizing him up, making judgments about the boy before he got to know him. Martin noticed it but did not linger on it.

"What took you so long?" Terrence asked Martin.

"I had to press my clothes, man. You know how it is..." Martin said with a smirk, pointing at the young man's basketball shorts. "Or, maybe you don't," he said with a laugh.

As Martin and Terrence exchanged playfully hard looks, the two strangers walked away, about twenty feet from where the others were standing. Martin, still looking at Terrence, nodded his head in their direction.

"Oh!" cried Terrence upon recognizing his gesture. "They're Michael's cousins."

"Oh... yeah." Michael chimed in. "Yeah, they're visiting us for the summer. My mom told me to take them with me. I didn't want to, but... yeah."

Martin looked over at the two. They were standing close to each other, talking quietly. As one talked, the very one who gave Martin the hard stare, the bigger, older one waved about in an exaggeratingly cartoonish fashion, jumping up and down, turning and twisting his head, and slamming his fist over and over into his open left hand. Suddenly, he raised his eyes toward Martin, who may have been staring a little longer than he had planned to, and gave him another hard stare. He ceased his animation, and kept talking to his younger brother, right into his ear, while still burning holes through Martin with his eyes.

"So, yeah, they were having a battle, and the boy *ripped him up!*" Martin heard faintly coming from his friends as he broke his gaze from Michael's cousins. He turned his head to listen to the conversation.

"He made Little Big G-sta look stupid! I'm tellin' ya!" Joey yelled excitingly.

"Awww... come on, man! You know Little Big G-sta's the better rapper. Nobody can touch him," replied Terrence. "And, besides, that Lil' Squiggly Boy, or whatever his name is, didn't even free style his rhymes. They were rehearsed! You could tell! He ain't never been that good!"

Just then the two cousins returned to the group and joined in the conversation. Martin stood by saying nothing, as he was upset at all the hard stares he was getting from the two.

"What are you all talkin' about?" asked Frank, the older of the two boys, the one who gave Martin the hard stares.

"Oh," said Michael. "We were talking about that rap battle between Little Big G-sta and Squiggly Boy. We watched it yesterday, remember?"

"Oh... yeah," Frank replied. Then, without regard to where in the conversation the boys were, he let out a loud, "Little Big G-sta ain't shit!" Then let out a heavy laugh, "Ha, ha, ha!"

Martin couldn't control himself. He was tired of the looks, and they had pushed too far with this sophomoric comment. "What the fuck man?!" he yelled at Frank. "Why you gotta' talk about him like that?!"

"He was just playin', man." Michael interjected softly so as not to arouse any further anger.

Martin began to breath heavily, he stuck out his chest, and squared up on Frank who was standing with his arms crossed, laughing at Martin's angry outburst.

"I wasn't joking," Frank said, each word slow and

deliberate. "I meant it. He... ain't ...shit!"

Martin's vision turned red as his heart began beating faster and faster. His hands, now both balled into fists, shook with intense anger. Without thinking, Martin leaped at Frank and began throwing fists at him; first his face, then his stomach, then back up to his face again. Martin was blinded by rage, and had no control over where his blows were landing. Then, from the side, the younger cousin, who was still older and bigger than Martin, jabbed his right fist dead into Martin's left eye. He fell hard, then lay unmoving on the dirt and grass.

A moment later, when he awoke, Martin looked up and saw Joey and Terrence standing over him with worried looks on their faces. He immediately raised his head to see if the two strangers were still there. Making sure he was not still in the middle of a fight, he scanned wildly, but saw only Joey and Terrence. While he was unconscious, Michael forced the two cousins back home. Martin began to calm. His breathing returned to normal, but his hands were still shaking. He rested his head back onto the ground.

"You all right, Martin?" Joey asked.

Martin nodded his head without lifting it. "Yeah... I think so."

"Man... they knocked you *out*!" Terrence said, hoping to get a laugh out of the boy.

Martin just looked up at him in disappointment. Terrence, who made the statement in jest, assumed a serious countenance, then reached his right hand down to Martin. Joey took the cue, and did the same. Martin then reached both of his hands toward theirs and grabbed them. Together, they lifted the defeated boy up.

At that time, the sun was beginning to set, and none of them were allowed to be out after dark. So, together, they all headed home. As they walked, and before they reached the corner where the three would separate and head to each respective house, Martin said, "You guys could have *at least* helped me."

Joey and Terrence looked at each other, then at him, and noticed a smile on his face. The three laughed. They joked about the fight, and about the dark spot forming around Martin's swollen eye, all the way until they reached the corner. They said their good byes, then each went on his own way.

"How am I gonna' explain this to Gramma?" Martin thought to himself as he walked down the block toward home.

VI.

Marlene woke up later that evening feeling an intense pain in her head. She felt as though some homunculus miner was inside, desperately trying to find gold. She was lying in a fetal position. She turned to lay on her back, then she rubbed her eyes which were sore from the warm saline tears that flooded from them while she slept. She reached out to her sides with her arms and pointed her toes toward the wall as she gave herself a quick, satisfying stretch. She always had a tendency to move her legs, alternatingly, up and down as she stretched. As she did, she felt again the odd slippery sensation between her thighs. She did not even think about it, but was instantly stricken with the same sinking feeling as before. She remembered how she felt earlier; being in her father's room, and running out crying. A churning began in her stomach and she got up and ran to the bathroom. As soon as she reached the door she felt it coming up. She threw the door open with her left hand while her right covered her mouth. She walked in, then slammed the door shut and instantly threw her face over the toilet. Her stomach cramped, twisted, and squeezed, yet nothing came. It did it once more, but still nothing burst forth. She knew she would feel better if she would just vomit, so when the squeeze came yet again, she forced it. A small amount of brown liquid fell from her mouth and into the cold water in the toilet. Once it was all out, Marlene sat against the wall opposite the cool ceramic bowl, her head rested atop her knees. She sat still and just breathed.

Marlene sat there for ten minutes, refusing to move any part of her body out of fear of intense pain. She decided that it made no sense to sit on the bathroom floor for the rest of the evening, so she raised her head to see if the pain had subsided. She did it slowly, at first, and there was no pain. She then moved it up quickly. Although slightly light headed, dizzy, there was no pain. Then she began to stand. As she did, she could feel a difference in her abdominal muscles. They were tight and a little sore. She shrugged it off, then walked to the sink, turned on the cold water and gently splashed handfuls onto her face and neck. She let the coolness of the clear water relax her. When she was done, she pat dried her face, then walked back to her room.

As Marlene was approaching her bedroom door, she heard the fain sound of her cell phone ringing. Panicked, yet excited, she hastened her pace. She flew through the door, shut it and locked it, then ran to her phone which rested on the floor near the head of her bed. She looked down and noticed that the phone was connected to the charging cable. "Odd," she though. "I don't remember plugging this in." Disregarding such a detail, she picked up the device and looked at the face of it to see who was calling. It was Andrew! With her thumb, she tapped the green button on the touchscreen.

"Hey," Marlene said after placing the phone snuggly against her ear.

"Hey," Andrew replied.

In the background Marlene could hear the sound of voices and cars rushing by.

"Did you get my picture?" she asked.

"Yeah. It was nice."

"Why didn't you reply back?" she suddenly snapped at him.

"I... uh," the boy stammered. "I just-."

"It's okay," she said, interrupting him gently. "I've been waiting for you to call all day."

"You have?" he said apologetically.

"Yeah..." her voice trailed off.

For a moment, neither said a word.

"What's wrong?" Andrew started.

"Nothin'. I'm just thinking."

"About what?"

"Nothing," A pause. "Hey, what are you doing tonight?"

"No plans," the boy replied.

"I'm gonna' come to your house tonight, okay?" she asked, unsure of his potential reaction, as she had never been to his house nor has she posed such a question and in such a direct fashion to anyone before.

"Okay..." the boy replied, unsure of exactly what he was supposed to say. "I'll be home around eight," he continued excitingly.

"Okay," Marlene replied.

Afterward, there was a moment of silence that came quite close to being awkward. Neither were sure of how to move on from this particular subject. Andrew wanted more details about the visit, yet Marlene wanted to be mysterious about her intentions. This could not be helped, as the girl was not sure exactly what her intentions were.

"So, what –?" Andrew began.

"Hey," Marlene interrupted. "I hafta' go. I'll see you at eight, okay?"

"Okay," Andrew replied, and before he could say good bye, Marlene reached her thumb back up to the face of the phone and ended the call. "How strange," Andrew thought after the conversation. "She was acting weird."

She was never the type of girl who followed popular culture closely. Marlene never wanted to be just like the other girls who, in school, rambled on and on about *this* celebrity or the new album by the new, beautiful pop star. She used to scoff at how her peers would spend long mornings preparing themselves to match closely their favorite super star; all just to show off to other *children*! No, she never wanted to be those people. Besides, even if she did her mother would never let her, as she was the one who bought her clothes, shoes, and the few accessories she was able to persuade the woman to buy for her. If her mother knew she dressed the way the other girls did, or wore makeup at all, she was certain she would never see the outside world again.

Marlene thought about all of this as she showered and then dressed. She put on an old pair of light blue denim pants, a small white t-shirt, and a pair of plain white flats. She then stood in front of the mirror in her bedroom. "I look like a child," she thought to herself.

"I wish I had some better clothes," she continued with a scowl. Suddenly, a new thought occurred to her, striking her, "Andrew said he wasn't home, didn't he? Well, he insinuated it. Hmmm… and it sounded like he was with other people. Maybe he was with another girl. One who didn't dress like a nine year old child! She's probably prettier than me, too." A deep sadness crept into her as she thought about her boyfriend with this possibly pretty, blonde girl who wore tight dresses and small underwear. Suddenly, her sorrow turned to anger, for Andrew should not be with a girl like that! He should be better than that! "That son of a bitch!" thought Marlene.

"What am I gonna' do?" she thought in a panic.

Then, in a fit of unusual rebelliousness, Marlene tore off her pants and threw them on her bed. She went into her closet and grabbed a small box. She opened the box, reached in and pulled out a pair of scissors. She then walked to her bed, took up her jeans, and began cutting. She decided that she did not want to cut them too high, then thought, "I'll bet that *girl* cuts them all the way up!" So, Marlene did the same. Once she had carefully measured and cut the legs from the pants, she slipped them on and walked back to the mirror. She stood for a moment evaluating herself. She looked at the cuts to see if they were even. They were, so she moved on to checking exactly how they looked on her, to see if they looked *right*. As she faced the mirror, she held in her stomach, then turned to see if her backside was showing. It was not, but came quite close. She was satisfied, and began to feel an unusual giddiness, almost on the verge of uneasiness, upon the thought of wearing something so forbidden. After her moment of self-scrutiny, she picked up her phone and snapped a picture. She sent it to Andrew with a caption, which read, "I can't wait to see you tonight ;)."

It was 9:45 pm, on an exceptionally dark summer night. Andrew was in his room pacing back and forth, wrenching his hands. "Where is she? I hope she understood the directions I texted to her," he thought to himself. Then, "Ack! She's not coming!" Suddenly, there was a knock on his window, a gentle rapping done softly enough not to arouse suspicion in whoever may be occupying the other rooms of the house.

Andrew jumped, started, when he heard the knock; more so out of tension and anticipation than fear. He ran to the window and threw open the curtains. He looked around, from left to right, but did not see anything but the darkness. "Was it my imagination?" he thought. Then a light shone. It was rectangular; "A cell phone!" thought Andrew. It shifted upward toward space, then, as it turned, slowly began to reveal a face. "She's here!" thought the boy ecstatically. Indeed, the light revealed Marlene's slim, young face. Her eyes darted back and forth, her eyebrows furrowed.

Upon understanding the message displayed in the nervous girl's fearful countenance, Andrew unlocked the window and slid it open. Marlene then walked up to the opening. She looked up at Andrew from below and with a sudden kind smile on her face, gently whispered, "Hey."

"Hey," Andrew whispered back, then put out his hands.

Marlene reached her hands out to his and grasped

them firmly. Andrew then carefully began trying to pull her up and into his room through the small three by two foot opening. As he pulled, Marlene did her best to climb in but it was proving rather difficult. She had ahold of his two hands, but she had to bring her entire body up another two to three feet in order to properly reach the window. She put her foot against the wall to try to produce some leverage, but when she pushed she slipped, and lost her grasp of Andrew's sweaty hands. The girl then took four steps back.

"What are you doing?" Andrew whispered loudly.

Marlene did not respond. Suddenly, she ran directly at the window and, when she reached it, she jumped. Her head and chest flew into the room, but the rest of her did not. With a crash, her upper abdomen fell hard onto the window sill. She did not scream, yell, or make any pain related sound. She just began kicking her legs, flopping her body like a fish until the rest of her made it through the window. Marlene flipped, flopped, and kicked until, finally, she dropped like dead weight onto the carpet in Andrew's room.

Andrew stood by with his mouth hanging open in astonishment. He ran over to Marlene as soon as she fell, keeping the same dumbfounded expression on his face. He then reached down and grabbed her by the waist and began lifting her with all his strength. Noticing that he was unable to lift her in such an awkward position, and in such an awkward fashion, Marlene decided to give him a hand by pushing herself up from the floor. Once she got to her feet, the girl began wincing in pain. She lifted her shirt to survey the damage. It was not bad, just a scratch, and the lingering soreness remaining from wiggling her body on the hard wood of the window sill.

"Are you okay?" Andrew asked in a most sincere tone.

Marlene looked up at the boy, then looked back down at her belly. Again, she looked at him, then let out a light chuckle.

"Yeah, I think so," was her reply.

Marlene lowered her shirt, then walked to the side of the boy's bed. She took a deep breath, then sat down. She then looked around, at all that encompassed his room. She wanted to remember every last detail of this night, and also take a couple of minutes to avoid Andrew, letting his anxiety build. Directly in front of her was a small desk, on top of which sat a closed lap top computer. On the wall above the desk was a poster displaying the planets of the solar system; the Earth, Mars, the sun, and the rest. To the right, across from the foot of the bed, was the door. Behind her stood Andrew who had just closed the window and redrew the curtains. She turned her head to see him. He looked strange, as if unsure of what to do.

"Oh, man!" Andrew thought to himself. "She's sitting on my bed! And look at what she's wearing! My goodness, those shorts! And the way she's looking at me right now, with her eyes so bright! Oh man! What should I do?"

Marlene placed the palm of her right hand on the bed right next to her, then patted it suggesting he take a seat. Andrew swallowed hard as he felt the perspiration forming on his forehead, in his hands, and under his arms. He walked over and, during the three steps trip, stubbed his toe on the bare carpet, and nearly fell before he reached the girl. Acting as if it did not happen, Andrew continued his trek, then sat down next to her. He turned to look at Marlene, and found her trying desperately not to let out a loud, mocking laugh.

After a moment of silence, and once Marlene stopped laughing at the boy, the girl suddenly rested her head on his shoulder. Andrew began to relax a bit as he felt the tender pressure of the girl's head resting comfortable against him. In a bold move, he decided to reach his arm around her, then pulled her closer to himself. As he did this, she willfully scooted over, nearer the boy. The two now sat in silence, her hip against his, her head resting on his shoulder.

Marlene sat, comfortable in her position, with her cheek caressing the shoulder of her boyfriend. She decided it was time. She decided that there was to be no words spoken to spoil the moment, no discussion as to whether or not somebody was ready. *She* was ready! So, without words exchanged between the two, Marlene lifter her head, gently pushed Andrew onto his back atop the mattress, then she straddled him. Andrew made his mouth form as if he had something to say, but before he could get a word out, Marlene brought her face down to his and began to kiss him. Andrew did not want to fight it. He kissed her back.

The two teenagers kissed, then caressed, then fondled. Their bodies crashed together and became two ships at sea caught in such a violent storm! Poseidon himself could not brave such a fury! Before they had realized what was happening, the night was over. They had let the influence of their minds, yearning to be free to do as adults do, take control of their actions. The urges forced upon them had turned to pleasures which were driven by passion and the anguish of living the very restricted, fragile life of a child on the verge of becoming autonomous grown individuals.

At daybreak, Andrew woke up quickly, suddenly, and reached around hoping to find his girlfriend there next to him. He kept his eyes closed as he reached and felt, but there was nothing but the rest of the bed. He opened his eyes to find no trace of Marlene, no sign that anyone but he was in the room. Then Andrew felt a breeze gently tickle the back of his neck. He turned to look at the window. It was wide open. The girl was gone.

VII.

It was a cool autumn day in late November. The sky was filled with rolling, dark clouds which were swelling, ready to release all of its water on any random town. There were no people out, as they anticipated a rain which never fell.

A sudden, bitter, cold breeze wrapped around Gramma as she walked to her mailbox to check the mail. She walked up to the small arched box and pulled it open. There was nothing. "I went all the way out here in this *cold* for *nothin'*!" she thought to herself. She shook her head as she closed the box. As she began turning her way back toward the house, she saw Jackie across the street just stepping out of her car. Gramma waved, not really noticing whether her neighbor caught the gesture or not. Jackie stopped dead, surprised, then waved back with a half grin developing on her face. Gramma stood looking at Jackie to see if she would come over for a chat. Jackie noticed her waiting and looking over intently, so she walked over.

"Hello there, Jackie," Gramma said with a big smile on her face.

Jackie could not help but smile back, just as wide. "Hello, Mrs. Johnson."

"You just comin' home?"

"Yes… well, no."

"Ah. Is it yes or no, sweetie?"

"Well, I've been home about half an hour. I've been in the car for…" Jackie's voice trailed off.

"I see," Gramma replied while looking sternly at Jackie.

For roughly fifteen seconds, the two stood in silence. Jackie, after Gramma's last statement, turned her head as if signaling that she did not want to say why she had been sitting in her car for so long. For a moment, Gramma studied Jackie. She saw in her a tension, nervousness, an inability to look her in the eyes. She seemed to be avoiding the subject.

"Won't you come in, join me for some tea?" she asked Jackie.

Jackie simply nodded her head, then followed Gramma to the house. As they reached the front entrance, Gramma held the door open for her neighbor. Jackie did not want to seem rude, so she bade the old woman to enter first. Gramma did not move, so Jackie gave up and went ahead in.

She had never been inside of the house before. Sure, she has on occasion spoken with Gramma, and more times than she can remember has waved a 'hello' to her. She had always wanted to know what it looked like, to see how the old woman and the boy lived. She had always imagined plastic covered furniture, an old tube-style television set with an old doily resting on top of it, and maybe a small coffee table surrounded by comfortable furniture, on top of which would sit an old candy jar filled with potpourri.

As Jackie walked in, she was taken aback, as her suppositions were shattered. Mounted on the wall was a rather large, brand new flat screen. Her furniture was modern, leather, and very obviously expensive; not an inch of plastic covered it. She had a coffee table, but it was covered with books. Opposite the door was a fireplace, above which was a mantle being weighed down by a multitude of photos of family members who the old woman likely had not seen in years.

"Have a seat anywhere. Get comfortable. I got water on the stove that should be boilin' by now. I'll go make the tea," Gramma quickly said to Jackie.

"Oh… Okay." was all that Jackie could muster as she scanned the room.

Jackie slowly walked to the big, black, leather love seat that sat near the door. As she walked, she surveyed everything, took it all in. She stood in front of the seat for a second and took a deep breath as if she was about to make a huge commitment which, at the very second she sat, she could no longer back out of. She sat down in a manner of one jumping into a cold lake. Immediately, the couch cushions wrapped themselves around her, comforting her all the way through to her very soul.

"What'll you have?!" yelled Gramma from the kitchen.

"Oh, um… Black!" Jackie replied.

There was a symphony of sounds coming from the kitchen. Glass clanking, sugar shaking, water pouring, and spoons ringing as the tea was being prepared. Once the noise stopped, Gramma walked in holding two cups of tea in two matching cups which were atop two matching saucers. She walked up to the coffee table, then placed the cups down gently on the only clear spot, right on the edge of the table.

"I put milk and sugar in yours, I hope you don't mind," Gramma said to Jackie.

Jackie picked up the tea and saucer as Gramma took her seat in the empty spot right next to her. She sat close, yet left enough space as to keep her guest from feeling uncomfortable. When the old woman sat, she let out a heavy breath of air, then turned and looked at Jackie with a smile. Gramma moved her eyes to the cup of tea in Jackie's hand, motioning with them that suggested that she try it. Jackie brought the cup to her lips and sipped. As she tasted, she shot her eyebrows up in enjoyment.

"It's good, huh?" Gramma asked with a laugh.

"Yes, very," Jackie replied.

Gramma had a satisfied look in her eyes, as if the world had suddenly fallen into balance. She then reached out and grabbed her cup, sipped, then slowly placed it back atop the saucer. She sat back, then looked around the table for a moment. "Ah!" she exclaimed, then reached out and grabbed a small, black remote control that was hiding behind a stack of books. She aimed it just below the television, then pressed a button. Jazz music began to play from speakers that were hidden from view; it was older stuff from the Harlem Renaissance era; maybe Miles Davis or Duke Ellington. Jackie could not figure who it was, but it was smooth and enjoyable.

For a moment the two sat sipping their tea without speaking. On occasion, Gramma would glance at Jackie and flash a smile at her. The old woman still seemed to be sizing Jackie up with her eyes.

"Did I ever tell you about my first husband?" Gramma started suddenly.

"No. Never," Jackie, who had never had any kind of deep conversation regarding Gramma's relatives, went along with the direction she was taking with the conversation.

Gramma sat with her eyes turned in contemplation toward the sky. "George was his name," she began. "I met him in about the mid nineteen-sixties. I was about sixteen, seventeen years old. I met him at a school dance, and he kept tryin' to take my hand, but I didn't let him. He was so smooth that night, though, and I eventually gave in." Gramma let out a deep laugh. "That very night, he kissed me. It was my first, you see? So, naturally, me bein' the fool I was, I thought I was in love the very second his lips touched mine.

"He became my boyfriend, and for the first year or so we got along well. We'd go to the park, the movies, and family reunions. Where he went, I always followed close behind. It was *rare* to see us apart. He was a couple years older than me, see? So, it didn't take long before he was out of school and needin' to find a job. He went out for about a month, lookin' for somethin', *anythin'!* A lot of people turned him down, but eventually, he got somethin' helpin' build up the railways near downtown. He would come home from work so tired from diggin', and pullin', and haulin' all day. I used to try to make him feel better when he finally made it back to the house after a long day of hard labor. I would have a bath ready for him, some dinner, and I'd rub his tired feet… well, if he was up for it.

"Things began to change though, when he moved out of his parents' place. He would be mad, just *angry*, when he got home. He was always tired, even on his days off. One day he started yellin' at me, tellin' me how hard life was, having to go to work and having to pay for everything. Eventually, he stopped coming home at the end of the day. He would come back, mind you, but he would come home *late*, and *drunk*! One night, I was sittin' and listenin' to some music on the radio. I had his dinner ready and a bath drawn, and he comes in drunk outta' his mind!"

Jackie sat listening intently to Gramma's story. She could tell where it was heading, and on the inside, she had her objections; she did not want to be lectured by someone who was almost a stranger. But, Gramma's words, and the way she spoke to the rhythm of the music, kept Jackie silently glued to her seat.

"He stormed through the door," Gramma continued. "His eyes bloodshot and yellow. He was yellin' somethin' about his boss tryin' to fire him, and sayin' it was *my* fault. He said that if I helped out around there, he wouldn't have to worry, he wouldn't have to drink. I was still in high school, so there wasn't nothin' I coulda' done for him. Just cook his food, run him a bath, and try to make him feel good, to please him.

"Well, he was yellin', drunk, and I stood up tryin' to tell him how foolish he was bein'. I didn't even see it comin', sweetie, I'll tell ya', the man's hand came up quick! And struck me in the eye! Then came another and another, 'till I was bruised and bloodied. I didn't move until he was finished. I tell ya', I was scared for my life," Gramma paused, then looked down at Jackie who was still fixed on her story.

"Wh-," Jackie began. "What did you do?"

"What do you think I did?"

"I... I don't know. What could you have done in that situation?"

"I'll tell you what I did. I got my butt outta there!" Gramma said with gravity.

"I see," Jackie replied, then sank her head into her chest, deep in thought.

"You see?" Gramma said triumphantly.

Jackie nodded her head. Then, for a moment, there was silence as the message Gramma was conveying to her neighbor sank deeply into her psyche.

"But, anyway," Gramma started, trying to change the mood of the room. "How's that girl of yours? She should be almost grown now; she's about the age of Martin, my grandson, isn't she?"

Jackie raised her head and gave Gramma an almost mocking stare.

"What is it, sweetie?" Gramma asked.

"Marlene, she's... my daughter. She's pregnant," Jackie replied.

Gramma's mouth flung open in awe. "My goodness!" she exclaimed. "Such a young girl and... and pregnant?"

"Yep," Jackie said disappointedly. "Five months. Well, about five and a half."

"Who's the father? If you don't mind my asking."

"Oh, no... no. I don't mind," Jackie paused, trying

to find the right words. "She won't say. We think it's this boy she was seeing, but, like I said, she won't say."

"My... goodness..." Gramma said again shaking her head in astonishment.

"Well, anyway, how's ... Martin? Is that his name, your grandson?" Jackie tried to change the subject.

"Awww..." Gramma began. "The boy's a mess. He's always out with his no-good friends, and when he's here he plays this awful stuff he *calls* music; he sings along to it too. Damnable stuff. He don't do his school work. Says he don't care for it, doesn't need it. I tell him about how hard it is out there in the world, but he don't listen to me, to age, to experience."

"Ah," Jackie said. "It must be hard with a boy. I couldn't imagine having to deal with it."

"He's nothin' compared to his mamma'. She was *so much worse*. I just hope this boy doesn't end up on the same path or, Heaven forbid, puts some poor girl on it," Gramma sulked.

The two again sat for a moment in silence. Suddenly, Jackie's cell phone made a noise. She reached in to her small purse and pulled it out. It was a text message from John, her husband. Jackie read the message, then looked up at Gramma and shook her head, "It's my husband, John. He wants to know where I am."

Gramma gave her a hard look. "Well, if you gotta' go, I won't keep you." Then she pushed herself out of her seat.

"Yeah, I better get going," Jackie said, then stood. "Thank you for... for the tea," she said with a smile.

Gramma smiled back. "Anytime, sweetie. You take care of yourself, okay?"

"I will," Jackie replied.

Gramma then pointed her hand toward the door, and Jackie followed. They both walked to the door, then Gramma turned the knob and pulled it open, showing her neighbor out. They both smiled at each other and nodded, then, almost reluctantly, Jackie walked through the doorway and out of the house. Gramma watched as Jackie walked to the end of the driveway, across the street, and into her own house. She then shut the door and went back to her tea and jazz.

VIII.

A few years had passed. Martin and Marlene were then 16 years old, and they were both in high school, yet neither of them attended the regular public school. Marlene, who had such trouble during her pregnancy, and while raising her daughter, had dropped out for a time, then began taking adult school courses to obtain her General Education Diploma. Martin, on the other hand, was still in a high school, just not the one he *should* be in. Instead, after being expelled for fighting, continuous truancies and absences, and low grades, he was sent to study at a continuation school, which met one Friday per week, and gave the students text books and worksheet packets to do at home.

Martin, having grown to near full adult size, which was enhanced in appearance by the little growth of hair he wore just above his top lip, was on his way to a friend's house. He had long since abandoned his old friends, who had different goals, different ways of viewing the world, while all Martin could see was his future as a rapper. This new friend, Jeremy, also dreamed of being a rapper or a music producer.

It was about eleven-thirty at night when Martin left the house. In fact, he was not there for long, as he had spent the rest of the day at another friend's house. He just popped in to Gramma's place to take a quick shower and put on a fresh set of clothing. He made sure not to get there too early, as he did not want to run into Gramma. The two had not been on close terms since the night Martin came home heavily intoxicated. He was at a party one summer night, having fun dancing and talking to all the girls who were in attendance. He had made the mistake of mentioning to a friend, whose name and face he cannot remember, that he had never been drunk before; he had tried alcohol, but never drank enough to get him *drunk*. As Martin was talking to some pretty girl, his friend stealthily walked up to him with a red plastic cup full of something that smelled like mango and coconut.

"What *is* this?" Martin asked the boy.

"It's a drink," then a pause. "Just drink it!" he said to him playfully.

Martin gave the concoction a careful sniff. It smelled good, sweet, and did not have the sting he had remembered from the last time he imbibed. He then brought the cup to his lips and carefully put his tongue into the liquid, taking just a small taste. It was good, and tasted just like it smelled. "Why not?" he thought to himself, then turned the cup over and in just a few seconds had swallowed down the entire glassful.

After a minute or two, Martin felt a warm sensation in his chest, but he did not feel dizzy or sick. In fact, according to what he could recollect, there no change at all besides the warmth. He asked the faceless boy to get him another, and he did. Martin swallowed that one down too. The boy who had brought him the drinks had anticipated such an action, and quickly produced another cup full and handed it to Martin. Again, he swallowed it down.

It did not take long for so much alcohol, which was later revealed to be simply peach schnapps, a little coconut water and mango juice, to take effect. As he continued talking to the girl, Martin began to notice how comfortable he was becoming just standing there, although his body felt like it wanted to rest on the ground. He did not realize, however, that his speech was slurring, he was changing the subject of the conversation constantly, and he followed just about everything he said with a smug, haughty laugh. After the girl inevitably broke off the conversation, Martin turned to walk away when a sudden, rushing, spinning dizziness grabbed him by the top of his head and pulled him hard to the ground. He did not even have time to brace himself, he just went down like a tree falling in a forest.

Martin remembered everything up to that point, besides names and faces, but nothing else. He woke up on the living room floor of Gramma's house. Later, his friends would tell him that they took him home right after the fall. They said he was fighting them from the moment they tried to lift him out of the dirt, and said they had to take the keys out of his pocket to get the door of his house unlocked; as soon as they opened the door, Gramma was standing there waiting. She told them to just leave him on the floor and she'll take care of it. They did just that, but Martin, who was still fighting decided at that moment to tell Gramma just how he felt about her.

"You know... you know!" Martin slurred at Gramma. "You know, you were never good to me! Or my *mama*!"

Gramma just stood looking at the boy with her arms crossed, not saying a word.

Martin made an attempt to look up at the old woman but he could not manage to raise his head. Instead, he twisted his body in such a say that he could look at her while still lying on the floor; his left eye was the only one open, and he struggled to keep it on Gramma.

"You are *old*, and *mean*, and you *never* believed in me! Never!"

After yelling that final word, Martin closed his only open eye and cringed in pain. Tears began to fall down his cheeks. Gramma still stood by, not saying a word, just shaking her head at the boy.

"My mamma was a *good* woman... but, but... you turned her bad! It was you... you *old*, *rotten* woman! She never loved you, and I don't love you, and I can't wait to leave this... this place..." his voice trailed off. He stopped speaking, stopped moving, and his eyes were tightly shut with tears falling from them; after a moment, Martin fell asleep. Gramma, understanding that the alcohol was saying all of those hurtful words, sat down on the couch and watched the boy sleep for just a couple of hours. She listened as his breath at times became labored, heavy, and deep. She watched him as he writhed, as he lay on the bare carpet. Then, he was perfectly still, his breathing normalized. Gramma, confident that her grandson was capable of making it through the night, went to bed. Since then, it has been hard for Gramma to look at him like the child she had raised alone; *she* raised, instead of the woman, her daughter, and the father, who were supposed to take on the responsibility of raising a child they brought into the world, and instead ran off, abandoning the boy.

Martin constantly tried to keep that night out of his mind and instead of confronting it, he simply decided it best to avoid it altogether by staying out of Gramma's way. Instead of talking it over, he stayed away from the house as much as he could, and that is why he was not home earlier in the day, and why he will be leaving once again.

As he reached Jeremy's house, Martin could smell the floral, skunky scent of marijuana flowing from every open crevice of the house. He stood near the front door for a moment and took a deep breath, as he did not feel right, he did not feel complete, as if something were out of balance. He brought his hand up and knocked on the door, but there was no answer. Martin, remembering that Jeremy's mother was at work at that hour, decided it would be forgivable for him to knock harder. He did, then noticed the button for the doorbell on the wall beside the door being bathed in lamp light from above. As he knocked as hard as he could, he also rang the doorbell as much as he could, and continued doing so for about twenty seconds until the door bust open.

"Yo! What is it?!" Jeremy began angrily, but upon seeing Martin his furrowed brows relaxed, creating a look of both sentiment and excitement upon seeing his friend.

"Martin! Hey, sorry man. You was knockin' like the police or somethin'… had me scared."

"Yea?" Martin replied. "With all that smoke comin' from the house, I'm surprised they haven't called the fire department yet." Martin said, gesturing toward the neighbors.

They both laughed as they walked into the house. Jeremy stayed behind for a quick second to close and lock the door, while Martin continued walking toward his friend's room. He could smell the scent of marijuana growing increasingly stronger as he approached the bedroom door. He had smoked marijuana before, but he did not enjoy it much. His friends had always asked him to smoke with them, but he never did, and besides, he considered himself more of a drinker than a smoker.

"Go ahead in!" Jeremy yelled to Martin as he walked by. "I'm gonna' grab some beers! I'll be right in!"

Martin simply nodded his head and continued toward Jeremy's room. As he came closer he could hear the thumping sounds of bass speakers, but no other music. Then, as he walked up to the closed door, he heard laughing within; familiar laughing. "Is that...?" Martin thought as he turned the knob and pushed the door open. He looked around and saw three young men he had never met before, and three young girls, one of whom he had. In fact, this particular girl was one who Martin had been seeing for the past couple of weeks. He was surprised to see her there, as she did not mention she would be at this certain place at this certain time.

Martin did not want to seem suspicious, so he put on a cheerful countenance. "Hey!" he said to a room nearly full of strangers.

"Hey! Martin!" said the girl he knew loudly, slowly, and with a wide smile on her face; her eyes, which seemed closed, were obviously forced shut by the heavy marijuana smoke.

"Hey…" Martin replied reluctantly. "Hey, Cinnamon," he forced his words yet made an attempt to seem nonchalant.

Martin then stood to the side of the room and took in the scene. Two of the guys, along with two of the girls, were sitting on Jeremy's bed talking about matters which Martin could in no way care less about. The third young man was sitting at a computer desk which was in the far corner of the room. Martin could not see what he was doing on the computer, as the boy's body blocked the view. Next to the desk was a small love seat, upon which sat Cinnamon. Suddenly, the boy on the computer stood up, turned to Cinnamon with a big smile on his face, then walked over and sat right next to her. Martin began to get upset. He stood there in the corner watching them. He saw how they looked each other in the eyes as they talked, how the boy inched his way closer and closer to the girl, and especially how she made no attempt at stopping his advance. Unless Martin was mistaken, he believed the girl had acted as if they had not been together recently, had never kissed, never made love. Suddenly the boy, who had inched his way close enough to the girl to be hip to hip with her, put his hand on Cinnamon's shoulder. Martin could no longer take it, such an insult to his manhood. He began to walk toward the two when, suddenly, Jeremy burst through the door.

"I got the beer, I got the booze!" he shouted happily. "Who's ready to catch a buzz?!"

Upon hearing this, Martin decided to let the insult go, for now. He turned to his friend and helped him with the drinks. He grabbed the beers and set them on the floor near the bed. Jeremy then placed several clear and brown bottles of alcohol near the beers, and walked out of the room, only to immediately return with a small, blue cooler that was filled with ice, and, on top of which, was a stack of red plastic cups. Jeremy walked in and placed the cooler down just inside the room, near the door.

"Okay everyone! I got cups, I got ice, and I got the booze! The rest is up to you!" he announced to the group.

Martin did not hesitate. He grabbed a cup, threw a few ice cubes into it, and poured some brandy over the ice. He shook the cup a bit in order to allow the alcohol to get colder faster, and once he was satisfied with the presumed temperature of the drink, he dumped the contents into his mouth and straight down his throat. Then, he went back to the brandy and refilled his cup, and again he poured the alcohol down. He would go on to do this four more times, one after another.

"You okay?" Jeremy asked.

"Yeah…" Martin was perplexed. "Why?"

"You look mad, man. And you keep looking at those two over there," Jeremy pointed his nose toward the love seat.

"Oh…" Martin replied. "It's nothin'."

"Alright, man," Jeremy said. "Let me know if you need anything, alright? You need another drink? How many have you had already?"

"I'm okay... I'm okay," Martin repeated, glancing back and forth from Jeremy to the love seat, then back to Jeremy again. "I've had about six of these, man. I'll be good."

"Alright, man," Jeremy paused and studied Martin's face. "Just... just don't go crazy, alright man?" he said, then laughed.

Martin laughed back, though insincerely.

Just then, as Jeremy walked away to talk to some other friends, Cinnamon and the boy stood up and walked toward the cooler of ice. They both grabbed cups. The boy filled his with ice first, then turned and went to the beers on the floor. As Cinnamon filled her cup with ice, Martin walked over to her.

'Hey," Martin said sternly, questioningly.

"Hey, Martin," the girl said happily, as if unaware of any wrongdoing.

"What are you doing?"

"I'm getting a drink, silly," she said slowly, playfully.

"That's not what I mean."

"Oh..." she paused to think. "Well, what *do* you mean?"

"I *mean*," he said with emphasis. "What are you doing sitting there flirting with that guy? I thought you were with me? I thought we were together!" Martin's voice began to raise.

Cinnamon looked at Martin with gentle, sincere, forgiving eyes. "Look... Martin—"

"Is everything alright?" the boy from the love seat interjected. "Is this guy bothering you Cin--?"

That was it. Martin could no longer hold in his anger, his rage and fury that had built inside of him. He turned to the faceless, nameless, nothing of a person and struck him square in the nose. The boy was hit, taken aback, but was not out of the fight. He took a step back, then lunged at Martin, who then stepped out of the way. The boy flew past Martin, then turned around and was instantly struck again, this time on his right eye. The boy fell over backward, almost losing consciousness, and once he hit the ground, Martin seized the opportunity to finish the fight. He had lost so many, he was sure to never lose another so long as he lived.

Martin quickly jumped on top of the boy, straddled him, and began to release a barrage of blows to the boy's head. The alcohol was affecting Martin in such a way that he could not feel how hard he was hitting the boy, nor did he feel any remorse for striking him so many times. The beating continued for about five minutes, long after the boy had stopped fighting back, stopped moving, and stopped breathing.

Martin then stood up and over the boy in victory. He looked around the room and was greeted with a group of terrified faces. Cinnamon, who had begun crying, was on her phone calling for an ambulance. Martin could not hear her, he could not hear anybody, although he could see their mouths moving. He then decided he had better go, to disappear for a while, and let this matter settle itself. He walked over the boy, opened the door, and walked out of the room, then out of the house, and finally around the corner to Gramma's for a quick shower and a change of clothes. Next, he would be off to some other friend's house to spend the rest of the night.

IX.

"Marlene, honey!" Jackie spoke gently into the door of her daughter's bedroom while knocking gently at the same time.

For a moment there was no sound coming from the room. Then, the door knob began to shake and then twist just slightly back and forth. Finally, there was a full turn, and the door was pulled open. A tiny child's head peeped out from behind; a head full of curly golden hair, and bright, inquisitive, green eyes.

"Gramma!" cried the little girl laughing.

"Hi, Andrea," Jackie said to the little girl with a warm smile. "Is your mama' in there? Can you tell her I have some lunch made for her and one special little princess?" she said with a raised voice so the person inside the room, if there was one, could hear.

"M'tay," the child replied to her grandmother, then stepped back and closed the door with a slam.

"Mama!" the child said as she approached Marlene, who was lying on her bed staring at the pattern formed on the ceiling.

"Yes, baby?" Marlene asked, suddenly broken from her spell.

"Gamma say, she has lunch."

"She has lunch?"

"Yeah."

Marlene took one second to think about the child's statement in an attempt to decipher the coded message of: "She has lunch."

"Gramma made lunch?" Marlene asked upon discovering the meaning.

"Yeah," Andrea replied.

"Oh! Okay," Marlene said. "Okay, baby. Go ahead and go get lunch, and mama will be out in one minute, okay?"

"M'tay," Andrea replied.

Marlene sat up and shifted her body onto the edge of the bed, swung her feet over, then stood up. She then took Andrea's little hand and walked her to the bedroom door, opened it, then gave the child a slight nudge in the direction of the kitchen where Jackie was scooping food onto plates and into bowls. Marlene then closed the door while still inside the room. She was not feeling quite hungry and did not feel like interacting with anyone. For the past couple of years, this feeling had come and gone, but for the nine months of her pregnancy with Andrea, and for the first year after her birth, Marlene became a shut in, so to speak. She would stay in her room at all hours of the day, except for the time when she needed food, or when she decided to shower. When those necessities came up, she would always open the door just slightly and listen for sounds, and if it seemed that all was clear, that nobody was around, she would sneak out and do whatever it was she needed to do. During her pregnancy, Marlene had to be just about dragged from her bedroom to go see a doctor regarding the health of her baby who nestled inside of her womb, unaware of what was happening just outside, helpless against whatever may happen to her, whatever nutrition she may or may not receive, whatever negative feeling affected her by way of a chemical change in her mother's body.

For the past year, however, since Andrea had begun to walk, talk, and show genuine human affection, Marlene has started to come out from that proverbial rock she had covered herself with. She began to come outside of the house every now and then, and had even built up the courage to start going back to school to get her G. E. D.

Marlene thought about this as she lay back on her bed, staring once again at the tiny lumps that covered her bright white ceiling.

Suddenly, Marlene's phone began to ring. Most often she would not even so much as acknowledge the menacing sound of her ring tone, ignoring the call, but this time, during a particularly rare occurrence, she rolled over and grabbed the cell phone which sat under her pillow. She did not recognize the number that was displayed on the face of the phone, but she decided, for reasons unknown to her, to tap the green button and answer the call.

"Hello," Marlene sternly stated after she put the device to her ear.

"Um… hello? Marlene?" a female's voice replied.

"Yes. Who may I ask is calling?"

"Marlene. It's Jessica."

"Jessica?" Marlene asked excitedly, as she suddenly

recognized the voice upon hearing the name.

Jessica was a good friend of Marlene's. The two had just about grown up together. They were in the same class in elementary school from first through sixth grade, and both went on to attend the same middle school. Marlene had not seen, nor talked to Jessica since she found out she was pregnant.

"Yeah," Jessica replied. "How are you?" she asked with a pure sincerity.

"I'm... I'm good," Marlene replied, matching Jessica's genuine tone. "How did you get my number? I've change it, like, four times in the past year!"

"Oh. I hope you don't get mad. I got it from your mom. I ran into her at the grocery store and she told me that I should give you a call."

"Oh," Marlene responded and followed with a short pause.

"Hello? Are you still there?" Jessica asked.

"Yeah, I was just thinking. Sorry," Marlene replied.

"Okay. So, yeah, how are you? Let's get together. We should go do something. There's a party tonight, we should go! Come on, we're both still young! You need to get out, girl!"

Jessica seemed to be rambling on and on into Marlene's ear. While her friend talked, Marlene threw in an "uh-huh" or two to keep from seeming rude. She tried to keep up with the conversation, but the weight of the subject was just too much. Thoughts of worse case scenarios popped into Marlene's head; who would babysit Andrea? What if she ran into Andrew or somebody else she knew but did not want to see? But, then again, Marlene thought about Jessica, her friend who she had not seen in so long. "It would be great to see her, talk to her," Marlene thought to herself. "And parties aren't *too* scary."

"Okay," Marlene said suddenly, not realizing where in the conversation the two were.

"What?"

"Okay. Let's go out. Let's go to the party. I'll ask my mom to watch my daughter."

"Okay, great. Amazing! I'm so excited! I can't wait! You still live at the same house?"

"Yeah."

"Yay! I'll come pick you up tonight at nine, okay? Is that time okay? I don't want to have you out too late."

"That's fine. Nine is fine," Marlene said, reassuring her friend.

"Okay, great! I'll see you then! We'll catch up then, okay?"

"Okay, yeah! I'll see you at nine!" Marlene said, then listened attentively to the sounds in the phone, waiting for something like a good-bye from her friend. None came, so Marlene pulled the device from her ear, then pressed the red button.

Marlene then threw herself from atop the bed, stood up, and walked out of her room, then straight to the dining room table where Jackie had Andrea seated in a booster char, eating macaroni and cheese and apple sauce, and drinking a box of orange juice. Marlene walked up slowly behind her daughter, bent down and kissed her on her head. Andrea looked up while chewing her food, saw her mother, smiled as best she could with cheeks full of pasta, and then turned back to her plate.

"Hey, babe," Jackie said to Marlene as she washed the pots and bowls used to cook the macaroni and cheese. "You hungry? There's more in the refrigerator. I can warm it for you."

"No. Thank you. I'm... I'm not hungry," a pause. "I'll have something later."

"Okay, dear," Jackie replied. "Hey, I thought I heard you talking in there. Did you get a call from someone?" she asked with a conspiratorial grin on her face.

"Oh, yes," Marlene replied. "It was Jessica, from school. Do you remember her? She asked me to go out with her tonight."

"I see," Jackie said, then paused. "So, are you going? I can babysit Andrea if you need me to."

Marlene looked up at her mother and smiled, convinced that everything had already been pre-arranged by her and Jessica. She then walked up to her mother, reached out both arms, and gently wrapped them around her, giving her a loving, tender hug. "Thank you, mom." Marlene said softly.

Jackie planted a kiss on the top of her daughter's head. "You're welcome, sweetie."

Marlene then released her hold of the woman, turned back to her own daughter and gave the girl another light peck atop *her* head, and walked enthusiastically, nearly skipping, to her bedroom.

It was about eight forty-five when Jessica arrived at Marlene's house. Marlene was not yet ready to go, so she asked Jessica to come into the house while she finished dressing. As her friend walked through the door, after Marlene's greeting, she was attacked by tiny Andrea. The child, upon seeing the guest, threw on a big bright smile, and rushed at Jessica, wrapped her arms around her legs, and laughed heavily and gaily as if she just met her favorite fictional super hero.

Marlene managed to pry her daughter from Jessica's legs, and, once this arduous task was completed, she invited her guest into her room, safe from Andrea's outrageous affection, while she finished getting ready for the party. Jessica accepted, and followed Marlene into her room, and once there she sat and watched as the girl stood in front of a full sized mirror and put her hair up into a little bun. Then, noticing how conservatively she dressed, Jessica suggested she try something a little more provocative, more modern. Marlene told her she had nothing like that in her wardrobe, which prompted Jessica to look through the girl's closet for something else, an alternate combination of garments which will make her seem as though she belonged at a party with people of her age. Jessica looked, and searched, and dug until she finally came across a pair of denim shorts, the legs of which had been cut quite high. She pulled them out of the closet, then threw them at Marlene. Upon seeing this particular pair of shorts, Marlene gasped, taken aback by the negative nostalgia. She picked them up and tossed them back in the closet, ardently refusing to put them on or see them again. Jessica did not understand what about those shorts disgusted Marlene so intensely, so she aborted her mission of trying to find an alternative to what she was already wearing. The two girls both agreed that the dark blue denim jeans, small black camisole covered by a light leather jacket, and a pair of black flats would suffice.

Once Marlene was dressed and fully adorned with the very few accessories that went along with her manner of dress (A small silver ring on her right ring finger), she kissed her daughter and her mother and followed each with a good-bye, then she and Jessica walked out to the small, black sedan that would take them to a two story track house at the edge of town. As they drove, Jessica behind the wheel and Marlene in the passenger's seat, the two young ladies caught up with each other on all that had occurred since last they spoke in middle school. They chatted about school, about people they knew years ago, who Jessica still saw and talked to but who Marlene had not and may never see again. They talked about little Andrea, life as a parent, and how terrified Marlene was when she found out she was with child. Marlene described to Jessica how she did not have the morning sickness that everybody seems to get in the movies, how long it took her to realize that she had missed her menstruation period (two months), and how she had decided to take a pregnancy test, and when she did how her heart sunk when she saw the two purple plus signs on the plastic stick. She went on to mention that she stopped talking to people for a long while, but decided not to reveal exactly why. Jessica, who did not have much to share beyond the trivialities associated with being an average adolescent in high school, could only sit and listen while Marlene disappeared into a world of thoughts and memories, fears and excitements, and then moments of happiness, of bliss, especially at the thought of the moment a friendly female nurse gently placed a snuggly wrapped Andrea into her arms and she knew for the first time exactly was it means to love someone.

Not long before the two reached the house where the party was being held, Marlene stopped talking and drifted into a thoughtful silence. Jessica felt more of a need to respect that silence than to make an attempt at breaking the awkwardness of it. As the car turned around the corner, the girls noticed that most of the block was full of cars, belonging, no doubt, to the home owners and party goers alike. Jessica decided to park farther down the street as there was open space available there. She drove until she found room next to the curb and, when she found it, she parked the car. Jessica then quickly pulled the hand brake beneath the steering wheel, and when she did, the rapid clicks of the apparatus brought Marlene back with a gasp, as if she was startled out of a deep sleep.

"Are you okay?" Jessica asked after her friend jumped at the sound of the brake being pulled.

"Yeah," Marlene said.

"I mean, we can go back if you're not ready for this."

"No… no. I'm ready."

Jessica then turned the car off, pulled down the sun visor, and flipped a plastic cover to reveal a hidden mirror. She looked into the mirror, studied herself to make sure her makeup was still as it was when she put it on earlier, then looked at her hair to see if any single strand had fallen out of place. A few had, so she very gracefully licked two of her finger tips and used them to gently push the hairs back into place. Conversely, Marlene did not pull down the visor nor look into any mirrors, but simply sat watching Jessica, and waited for the cue to open the door and get out of the car.

Finally, after about five minutes of pushing, pulling, reapplying, and fixing, Jessica gave Marlene a look and a smile signaling that she was finished and ready to go. Marlene replied with a single nod of the head, then they both almost simultaneously stood up and out of the vehicle. They both gently closed the doors, then made their way down the street to the house from which music can be heard from where the girls were standing on the opposite end of the block.

The girls arrived at the house at around nine forty-five. For the first two hours, everything went well. As they entered, Marlene quickly grabbed ahold of Jessica's arm, as she was much more nervous about being in such a social situation then she had imagined. Jessica, with Marlene in tow, managed to walk through just about the entire house, talking to one random stranger, then another, and introducing Marlene to friends who Marlene had never met before. The two were also able to run into old friend and acquaintances from their elementary and middle school days. Marlene did not remember a lot of them at first, but when she heard their names, she immediately realized that she was talking to the same child she knew in the past who had grown in height, weight, and age, with faces that had filled out or sunken in from growth and time.

Eventually, Jessica, who had been drinking from the moment she entered the house, had persuaded

Marlene to imbibe. She drank just a little at first, and what she drank was heavily mixed with concentrated fruit juices. Later, she would gulp down a couple more mixed drink cocktails and one or two shots of an unidentifiable, burning liquid. Once the alcohol began to take effect, Marlene found the strength to release the colossal clench she had on Jessica, and the courage to peruse and mingle alone. She met back up with friends from the past, caught up with them, talked about life, and joked about particular events that had occurred to them mutually when they were children.

At one point during her exploration of the house, and her inquisitive investigation of all who inhabited it at the moment, she came across a young man who she thought she knew, but did not altogether recognize, as though he was someone she had met a long time ago, but had forgotten, or had seen in passing in some random setting in the not too distant past.

"Hey!" Marlene, feeling loose, said to the young man freely.

"Hey," He replied in a disconnected fashion, trying not to engage in a conversation with her.

"You look familiar. Do I know you from somewhere?" she asked.

The young man gave her a hard look, then turned his head avoiding the question.

"Alright..." Marlene said peevishly, then turned away to move on to the next potential long lost friend from the past.

The boy tuned back and watched the annoyingly intoxicated girl walk away. He kept the same hard look on his face as he shook his head disapprovingly at the tipsy young girl. Suddenly, the young man's friend walked up and noticed him staring at Marlene.

"Hey, Martin. You know her? She one of your ex-girls?" he asked.

"No," he replied indifferently. "I think I used to go to school with her; long time ago."

Martin's friend said nothing in reply, but simply nodded his head in understanding. He then turned around and picked up two plastic cups which he had placed on a small table and handed one to Martin, who then lifted the cup to his mouth and poured the contents down his throat. Once the cup was empty, Martin winced.

"What is that?" Martin asked.

"Straight whiskey, boy!" he yelled proudly. "You drank it all?"

"Yeah," Martin said, then held out his hand. "Give it to me." he told his friend who then handed him his cup and watched in awe as Martin threw down another cup of whiskey.

"Damn, man! You gotta' take it easy. It's still early!"

"Nah, man. This is nothing. I'll be alright," Martin said as he wiped the remnants of the whisky that had spilled out from around his mouth with the back of his hand.

His friend stood in amazement, shaking his head at the foolish act of his friend, Martin, who himself believed the actions to portray brevity, as proper, perfectly fitting the behavior of a *real man* when confronted with large amounts of alcohol. Martin's friend then took the cup from Martin's hand and headed back into the kitchen to fill another for himself. Martin, not yet realizing that his friend was not returning with more alcohol for him, stood waiting, feeling the alcohol quickly buzz through his head and face. He began sinking into his own mind, remembering the day when he was a child in elementary school with that girl whom he recognized immediately. He did not say so, as he did not want to engage in a conversation what that evil, vile girl, who had once defeated and embarrassed him in front of the entire class. He remembered then how many times his classmates made fun of him for sobbing pitifully as Ms. Rodinsky held him back. He remembered Marlene's haughty look of satisfaction as she stood beyond his reach, beyond his vengeance. Suddenly, a thought occurred to him, "I know what I'll do." He could feel the alcohol beginning to take a strong hold over him. "I'm gonna' go find that girl. I'm gonna'… gonna' talk to her… real sweet. Then, I'm gonna' seduce her. I'm gonna' have sex with her. I'm gonna' do her then leave her there feeling like a fool. I'm gonna take back what she stole from me; my dignity, my respect, my ability to be taken seriously, like a man *should* be. I'm gonna' fuck her and forget her, just like Little Big G-sta said, like a pimp!"

Suddenly, Martin awoke from his daydream and began looking around the room for Marlene. He did not see her there in the living room where he stood, so he proceeded to search the entire house for the girl who, a long time ago, made him look foolish.

For a while he searched, in the kitchen, in the backyard, the front yard, and each room one by one for Marlene. As he looked, and the alcohol flowed through his system, he thought more and more of the moment when he would get back at this girl. But as time passed, he began to think more about the sensations associated with the impending event than with the psychological freedom he expected to feel upon having his vengeance. He thought about the smoothness of her soft body, filled out from puberty and pregnancy, curvy and voluptuous; about kissing tenderly, and speaking gently into her ear sweet compliments and promises which he had no intention of keeping. His desperation grew stronger with the aid of the tactile lust he began to feel for the girl.

For thirty minutes the hunt went on, and Martin was not able to find Marlene. He decided to take a short break and headed to the kitchen to fill another cup of whiskey to gulp down. He walked into the kitchen with his head down, lost in his feverish thoughts of lust and vengeance, and straight to the cups as if he was being controlled from some outside power. He then took the cup to the alcohol in much the same fashion. The boy placed the cup atop the kitchen counter, grabbed a bottle of nearly empty whiskey, and unscrewed the cap. He turned the bottle over to pour, and the brown liquid rushed out and into the awaiting cup below. Once the cup was full, and coincidentally the bottle empty, he picked it up and poured it down his esophagus, just as he did with all the others. As he took his last swallow he gagged just slightly, then a voice called out to him.

"Martin?! You're Martin, right? You went to Marshall Elementary? Ms. R's class, third-grade? I'm Marlene. Do you remember me?" she asked Martin, voice wavering, speech slurring, yet with a gentleness in her eyes and smile.

Martin became angry at the sight of her. "How dare she just walk up to me and pretend that we never fought, acting like she's such a nice person! What a bitch!" Martin thought, then remembering he had a plan to get her back, he put on a smile worthy of the best used car salesman.

"Yeah... yeah! I remember you!" he said with a laugh. "Marlene, right? Yeah, Ms. R's class! How are you?" he asked the girl utilizing his best acting skills.

Marlene looked at him awkwardly. If she had not been drinking she would have taken his suddenly assumed smile as a joke, as if he was mocking her when she was just trying to be friendly. "I'm good. I'm doin' good." she said, the paused to study his face. "How have you been?"

"I'm alright," he coolly replied.

After their brief reintroduction, Martin asked Marlene if she wanted a drink. She said no, but Martin persisted and persuaded her to have a small amount while they went into the living room to talk and reminisce. She agreed, but with caution. With drinks made and in hand, the two walked into the living room from the kitchen and found a heavily cushioned love seat in the middle of the floor. They sat down and, for a moment, said nothing to each other, but as they drank both had managed to exchange short glances at each other.

Finally, Martin began his scandalous siege by asking her about all she had done since their days in Ms. Rodinsky's class. He made sure to listen attentively, provide short, affirmative feedback, and to look her in the eyes while she spoke. While the girl went on about her life's hardship and happiness, Martin slowly, gently moved in closer and closer to her and, in time, found himself right next to her, so close he could smell the scent of the fabric softener on her clothing. Then, after Marlene had finished talking about the complexities of her life as a single mom, she realized that Martin was staring *too* intently into her eyes. He was smiling such a slim, devilish smile. Then, before she had time to think of his possible intentions, Martin leaned in and kissed her. The alcohol in Marlene's system kept her from panicking, from resisting. She kissed him back. Suddenly, she began to feel Martin's hand on her knee, and felt as it slowly travelled upward toward her most private area, one which had not been touched since the day Andrea was born.

Marlene, while still locked in a passionate kiss with Martin, put her hand on his to keep it from going any farther. Martin tried to push, but she refused to let him go higher. He was not trying to be gentle. He had a plan and he was going to follow it no matter what. He pushed hard without regard to her resisting. Marlene gasped as he reached between her legs, then immediately stopped kissing him and grabbed his arm.

"Don't." she said softly to prevent potential aggression.

Martin paid no mind to her refusal. He thrust his hand forward and began rubbing her. He pushed his lips toward hers in an attempt to resume kissing, but she pulled back and, faced with no other option, Marlene reached her open hand back then brought it forward fast and hard, right into the side of his face.

Martin did not take time to think about what he did

next. He did not plan it, nor did he know exactly what he was doing, but with ferocity and rage, Martin thrust his fist into Marlene's face, over and over. She screamed, shrieked as the boy laid blow after blow upon her. He punched, again and again, into the mouth, nose and eyes of the girl who had wronged him and had the audacity to reject him and even slap him! He punched fists forward and brought back bloody hands, until a crowd of partygoers pulled him off of the poor girl who had fallen to the floor, face bloodied, her swelling eyes peering up at the monster who had just attacked her. Martin roared like an animal, with wild eyes that seemed to glow in the dim light of the living room.

The crowd, with great effort, pulled Martin away and outside to the front yard, where he would fight his way from their grasps and then run ferociously, feverishly into the dark of the night.

Inside, Jessica had run to Marlene to comfort her. She had instructed some onlookers to call the police; one girl did while the rest gazed in stupefaction. In roughly five minutes the police, a fire truck, and an ambulance, which transported Marlene to the hospital, showed up at the house. She had suffered a broken nose, jaw, collar bone, and the crippling shame associated with being mauled by another human being, who beat her and left her, confused and bloody, to be gawked at by a crowd of drunken teenagers.

X.

A few days had passed since the terrifying day of the party where Martin lost himself to his animal needs and lusts for vengeance and ferociously assaulted poor Marlene, who never would have expected such an act to occur to her at any point in her life. The day after the incident, Gramma was at home when Jackie arrived from the hospital, where she picked up Marlene who was recently discharged. Gramma was in her front yard doing a little maintenance, trimming the leaves on the small bushes that lined the front of the house, and picking up garbage that seemed to accumulate beneath the very same shrubbery, when the car pulled up across the street. She witnessed as Marlene slowly, painfully pushed herself from the passenger's seat with the aid of her mother. Gramma decided then that it was not a good time to inquire, as it would seem as if she were meddling, hunting for information about which to gossip.

Three days after Marlene's return from the hospital, Gramma decided to go across the street to her neighbor's house to see if everything was okay. She did not want to seem as if she were prying, so to assuage any negative thoughts she baked a small yellow cake to take over, along with some of the tea she had served Jackie once before. Once the cake was ready, and the tea placed into one small re-sealable plastic bag, Gramma headed over. She gathered up the cake and tea, left the house, and walked across the street to Jackie's. Once she reached the door, she placed the bag of tea on top of the cake, which was not frosted, and pressed the button for the doorbell once. She then stood patiently, waiting for any sign of life.

Suddenly, breaking the silence of the neighborhood, the house, and the old woman who stood lost in thoughts about what could have happened to the poor young Marlene, the door flew open with a whoosh. There, in the doorway stood Jackie, smiling, happy the old woman came over to visit.

"Hello, there," Jackie said, greeting her neighbor.

"Hello, dear," Gramma returned the salutation with a sympathetic smile.

"Won't you come in?"

"Thank you," Gramma said as she walked into the house.

Inside, it was quiet, cold, and lonely. Gramma felt it eerie, as there was a small child who lived within, yet there were no signs of it, no sounds of laughter, no dolls or princess stickers miscellaneously attached to the walls. Jackie escorted Gramma into the living room where the recliner had been removed and replaced with a rather large, cream colored sofa that could easily fit five people the size of Gramma. Instead of the television set, there was now a coffee table that ran the length of the sofa. Gramma looked sternly at the entire set up , then decided to walk to the far end of it all and take her seat there, as she always felt most comfortable sitting as close to the center of the house as possible; it made her feel less like a stranger, no matter where she happened to be. She then gently placed the cake and bag of tea on the table in front of her. In the background, Jackie could be heard walking to and fro, stepping heavily, determinedly, as if she was in a hurry. Gramma could hear it all. Then came the sound of plates being stacked and silverware being placed atop the dishes. Then, the heavy steps began coming closer and closer to Gramma, until Jackie appeared and maneuvered her way around the end of the sofa, holding a small tray which held plates and forks for the cake, and a small tea pot full of hot water, and tea cups, and every other necessary item related to tea and cake and the consumption of each. She very carefully placed the tray of fragility down upon the table next to the items Gramma had placed previously. Jackie then poured water into the tea cups, placed one in front of Gramma and one near her intended seat, then she sat.

"Please, help yourself," Jackie said to Gramma, who then pulled her tea from the bag, opened each package, and placed two tea bags into her small ceramic cup to seep.

Jackie pulled out a tea bag from the pocket of the sweatpants she was wearing; it was a mix of black and raspberry flavored tea. She then placed the bag into her cup and dabbed it up and down while holding onto a string which extended from the small paper bag.

For about thirty minutes the two women sat chatting about how they were, what they have been doing with their time, how work was going, all the while sipping their tea and munching on forkfuls of yellow cake. Jackie mentioned how astounded she was that the yellow cake, although bland and boring in nature, was incredibly moist and sweet, and asked, if Gramma was willing, if she could get the recipe for it. Flattered, Gramma told her she would write it down and bring it over one day, then mentioned how wonderful the house looked, how amazingly clean and quiet it was. For thirty minutes the two engaged in this type of flattery and small talk until the tea was finished. That was when Gramma decided it was time to get to the real questions, to find out what was happening in the house that rested quietly across from hers.

"Listen, sweetie," Gramma said to Jackie with sincerity and seriousness. "I was at home a few days ago when you got home with your daughter. I saw how she was all wrapped up in bandages and slings and casts, and how you had to help her out of that car of yours. Now, usually I don't make it none of my business to ask about the private lives of others, but I like you, Jackie, and when I like somebody I feel concern for them and their families just alike. So, when I see that girl comin' outta' that car in pain, I told myself that I need to go over there and make sure everything was okay." Gramma looked at Jackie, who looked back at the old woman like a small child who had just been caught in a lie.

"It was all my fault," Jackie said as she sobbed. "If I hadn't been so *insistent* that Marlene get out of the house, *none* of it would have happened. If I didn't push her, and just let her take her time to come out and be with the rest of us, to be herself again…"

"It's not your fault, sweetie," Gramma said to comfort Jackie. "Now, what happened?"

"Well," Jackie took a deep breath, then continued. "She didn't tell us much; me or the police. She didn't say anything to the doctors. But, what she *did* say was that she was at a party with a close friend of hers from school, and they were drinking alcohol; she didn't want to lie, they took a blood test and found it in her system. She said that she was going around talking to people she knew, and some people she didn't know. Then, this guy, she said she didn't know him, tried to touch her… inappropriately," Jackie paused as she lost herself in the thought of someone touching her daughter, derailed by the anger that began to boil inside of her, but managed to continue. "She got mad, and pushed the guy off. But he wouldn't stop, so she slapped him. And then… and then…" Jackie trailed off again, fighting tears from forming in her eyes. "And then he just… *beat her*! She said she didn't know how many times he hit her, but it was a lot. She said she screamed for help, but it took a long time for somebody to pull him off of her. The police officer in charge of the investigation asked what he looked like, but she said she didn't remember. They think it's because of the alcohol; they say she was blacked out."

For a moment, the two women did not say a word. Jackie just sat and sobbed while thinking about how she could have prevented it all, while Gramma gently rubbed circles in Jackie's back in an effort to comfort the distraught mother.

"Listen, honey," Gramma started. "Nobody in this

world deserves to be treated the way your girl was treated. And I *know*, if all is *right*, and *God* is fair, and you are *faithful* to Him, everything will be okay. And they'll get that despicable creature who hurt her, I guarantee you that. I'll keep you all in my prayers," Gramma finished.

Jackie looked up at the old woman, tears falling from her eyes. "Thank you," she said as she wiped her cheeks with the back of her hand.

Suddenly, as the two sat weeping and comforting one another, the sound of screeching tires was heard extremely close by. Sirens, which were heard by the two moments ago, but were such a common sound where they lived that they paid them no mind, were sounding off loudly and in multitude. Gramma's heart began beating quickly, intensely, her chest heaved up and down, and a sudden emptiness gripped her soul. Quickly, she stood up and ran to the door. Jackie followed close behind. Gramma threw the door open to the view of a panorama full of police cars in front of her house, and officers kneeling at the side of their vehicles, guns drawn and aimed at the open doorway.

XI.

There was a strange, foreboding emptiness in the air that day. No people were in the streets, and there were very few cars in the roads. A simple, cool breeze blew from the North, which gently pushed leaves and empty potato chip bags from one point to the next with a gentle rustle. The sky was overcast, filled with an array of clouds of various shades of black and white, none of which seemed to be moving along with the wind. On this particular day, Martin found himself walking the streets alone, lost in his mind, not paying attention to anything in front nor behind him. He was wearing a black hooded sweater, black denim pants, and a black pair of running shoes that were almost completely covered by the ends of his pant legs. His stomach began to ache at the instant the smell of rain and damp concrete hit his nose. It was not raining where he was, but the thought of its inevitability made his hunger worse, and he decided then that he should find somewhere to get food before the rain fell and his day became as depressing as the dreary sky.

Immediately, Martin began to walk in the direction of a small gas station that was not far from where he then was. The food would not be great, but it would be something to silence the growls and alleviate the pains that were cutting through his stomach and intestines. Weeks before, he did not have had to worry about food, as he had friends who would have gladly taken him in and shared what they had with him, but Martin had long since torn apart the bonds he had made with so many people that the option no longer existed. Also, his belief that he had offended his grandmother beyond reconciliation had driven him far from the thought of ever going back to the house. So, he walked to the gas station to buy what he could with what little money he had.

It did not take him long to get there. He had walked for roughly five minutes before he reached the refill station that had only two pumps, old wood paneled walls that had blue and yellow paint chipping from every inch of them, and one attendant who happened to be the establishment owner's son, who sat inside of the small blue and yellow shack and sold within cigarettes, beer, sodas, and various preprocessed, prepackaged baked goods that were covered in sugar.

Martin walked through the single glass door. A small bell jingled as he entered. He looked toward the cash register where the attendant sat rifling through a magazine of some sort, switched over to his cell phone to type a quick text message, then went right back to the magazine. He saw Martin come in, but did not feel the need to acknowledge him.

For a few minutes, Martin browsed around the small store, examining the items on each shelf, down each aisle, though few there were. Over the course of his perusing, Martin was able to pick up a few items that piqued his interest. He knew they were what he wanted, as his stomach gave a low moan at the very sight of them. In his hands, he held two honey buns, a small pack of powdered doughnuts, a candy bar, and a bottle of fruit juice. He took the items to a back shelf, placed them down atop the counter, and reached into his pockets in a desperate search for money, hoping he had enough to purchase the items that would bring about his satiety.

Martin's search revealed a heavy lack of funds, as the items' cost would reach roughly five fifty-five, yet he had in his pockets a mere three twenty-seven. Immediately, he became distraught at the thought of not just having little money, but also that there were no alternatives at his disposal. He *had* to eat, and *these* were the items he wanted, and *this* was the store from which he wanted to get them. He had to do something to keep the pain from tearing him apart. Just then, Martin scanned the store to see where the attendant was, if anybody else was there, and if there were cameras anywhere in the place. He saw no camera, no other people, and the clerk still had his face buried deep within the pages of the magazine. Feeling that all was clear, Martin shoved the two honey buns and the candy bar into the front of his pants, in a place where his shirt would be just long enough to cover the new, unusual bulges formed by the hidden items. Martin then took a deep breath. His heart was pounding ferociously and off beat as he picked up the bottle of juice and the pack of powdered doughnuts, turned toward the front counter and walked as naturally as he possibly could to the cashier. As he slowly marched, Martin suddenly realized the attendant was not at the front counter. He had just seen him seconds before flipping through pages, but he had somehow vanished. Martin crept up to the counter and looked around, left, right, and stood on his toes in order to get a peek behind the counter to see if the man was hiding somewhere below. Suddenly, the clerk appeared at the door. In his hand was a shiny silver revolver, aimed directly at Martin. In a panic, the boy nearly jumped over the counter, but his fear kept him where he stood, shaking, eyes wide, sweat forming on his head.

"Don't... fucking... move..." the clerk said to Martin.

"Hey, man. I didn't do nothin'," Martin whimpered.

"Never mind that. Just don't you move. I don't wanna' have to use this thing."

"Come on, man." Martin said desperately as the attendant gently locked the door, then slowly crept over to the telephone which sat at the end of the counter near the door, and called the police.

"Hello? Yes, I have this guy here who's tryin' a steal stuff from my store. Yes. Yes, that's it. I don't know if he's armed. Uh-huh. Okay," the attendant said while Martin stood, frozen in place with his hands up, listening.

"Man, I didn't take nothin'!" Martin exclaimed as the man hung up the phone.

"Yeah? What's in your pants, there?"

Martin did not respond. He just stood there staring at the muzzle of the hand gun that was being aimed directly at him, praying in his mind that nothing happens, that this crazy guy does not pull the trigger and end his life.

Martin started thinking about his life. He thought about all the fights, the friends he had lost one way or another, the girlfriends who said they loved him yet left him for some other boy. Then, he thought about Marlene, sitting with her child, face deformed from punches that should have never been thrown. Suddenly, the thought of his own mother popped into his mind. All he had to go on was a photo from her teenage years, which Gramma kept on the mantle above the fireplace. Then his thoughts turned to Gramma. He thought of her smile, her courageousness, and her love. He thought of the way she would tuck him in at night, and would never get mad at him no matter what he did. He thought about how he had wronged her the night he came home drunk, and how he wished he was man enough to ask her forgiveness. Then, as Martin stood there, a simple flinch away from severe injury or death, the thought of Gramma running through his mind, tears began to stream from his eyes, becoming the dark grey clouds which hung low in the sky.

"It's too late now," The attendant said as he saw the boy begin to cry. "The police are comin', and you'll be doin' time for tryin' a steal from me!" he yelled, waking Martin from his watery eyed spell.

Sirens were suddenly heard in the distance. There were quite a few of them, too many to count by just listening. The gas station attendant figured that it was a good time to unlock the door, giving him an escape should Martin have a weapon. Martin saw the clerk turn just slightly to unlock the door. It took a while, and looked as though he was having trouble turning the mechanism. Martin then suddenly rushed forward, taking the clerk's inability to master the lock as an opportunity to run, to burst through the door and flee to safety.

"Damn!" the clerk let out a curse, then lowered the gun just for a second, and as it fell he was abruptly knocked to the ground as Martin threw, with extreme force, his entire body into him.

The pistol fell from his hands, and Martin used the time it took to recover the weapon to unlock the door himself. He reached down and turned the semi-circular key beneath the door handle, which instantly gave in to Martin's determined effort, then thrust himself through the glass door and outside, where police cars were just arriving.

As he exited the store and saw the first police car pull into the lot of the gas station, Martin, in a panic, quickly turned left and ran toward the back of the building. Immediately, he was met with a six foot tall metal fence which he very easily threw himself over. He hit the floor and took up his sprint as if there had been nothing at all there, no barrier for him overcome.

Martin did not realize where he was running, as he had no plan, but he knew that if he kept his feet moving he certainly would not be caught and thrown into prison. For miles he did not stop, as everywhere he went, at each turn, each move, no matter which direction he ran, the wailing of police car sirens seemed to be following him, matching his every step. He decided to come up with a plan, so he ran into a nearby narrow alleyway. He slowed his sprint to a light jog as he entered the alley, then spotted a dumpster that would prove to be an excellent source of concealment from the main street. He slowed to a walk as he approached it, and was stricken with the smell of years of garbage accumulation which attached itself to the bottom inside.

"What am I gonna' do?" Martin thought to himself as he squatted next to the metal dumpster. "I can't go anywhere. Nobody will take me in. Nobody's gonna' help me."

As his mind was engrossed in thought, a cool breeze rushed across his face, cooling the sweat and tears that were now dripping from his face. He wiped his eyes, then rested his head on his knees. A few more tears squeezed their way out of him as his body shook out of fear, desperation, and an overwhelming feeling of helplessness. He knew then that there was only one place he could go, one person who would take him in and protect him, treat him like a person in need. He did not want to be caught, and he had to move or they would eventually find him there, so he decided that it was time to go home, to seek shelter in the bosom of his grandmother, despite the utter disappointment she may feel about his actions.

The boy took a deep breath and clenched both fists as hard as he could. Then he exhaled slowly. Martin looked around to get a sense of where he was and, as he surveyed the area, he could still hear the sirens in the distance. He recognized where he was and realized that he was not far from the house, so he set off, not sprinting but jogging, quickly into the street. He ran down the block, took a left around the corner, went down and took a right, and there he was greeted by several police cars flying in his direction. Martin suddenly felt his feet take off, his heart tearing through his chest, his lungs ready to collapse. He turned around, ran back and took a right onto the street from which he just came. He took another right on the next block and sprinted as fast as he could to the end of it. Then, he took one more right and ran halfway down the block where Gramma's house sat waiting for him, welcoming him. As he reached the door and pulled the keys from his pocket, a low howling of tires sounded from the corner. Martin looked up and saw a police cruiser racing toward him. He shoved his key into the locking mechanism and turned it and the entire door knob, shoved the door open, then ran inside, leaving it wide open. He did not look around for anybody, nor did he call out for his grandmother. He simply ran into his room then closed and locked the door.

Upon entering his room Martin began to pace back and forth, tears still falling from his eyes, his head hot and covered with sweat. He reached into his pants and pulled out pastries and a melted candy bar, then threw them into the corner near the computer desk. Then he continued to pace, no thoughts running through his mind, just waiting to see what was to come next.

Martin looked around his room in an attempt to take it all in before the inevitable happened, before he would be prevented from seeing it again for possibly years. He looked at all the posters of his favorite rapper, the computer desk which was now bare as he had sold his computer and speakers long ago in order to buy some food, some alcohol, and a new pair of sneakers. All that remained was a photo he had long since forgotten about, of him as a child, eyes shining, smile as wide as the Pacific Ocean, without a care in the world or thoughts about the future. Martin walked closer to the desk. It was not a school photo, but one taken in church. He used to go every Sunday with Gramma, but he never enjoyed it, so she never made him come any other time she went. In the background of the photo was a large white cross that seemed to be glowing behind him.

The boy took a long, deep breath. A look of resolution came to his face as he gently placed the photo face up onto the desk top. Then he walked to the side of his bed, got down on both knees, put his two hand together, and began to pray.

"Lord," Martin started, unsure of how to begin as he had never actually said a real prayer in his life. "I know... I know I haven't been good. I've done a lot of bad... of *really* bad things. I know I hurt a lot of people, and I shouldn't have," he paused. "And, I know I don't deserve forgiveness. But, can you please... please Lord... please help me out. I..." Martin began to sob heavily, his breath squeezed from him as tears dropped from his eyes. "I just don't wanna' die, Lord. Please. Please! I'll be good, I'll never hit another person... and I'll never disrespect... my Gramma again... I swear. Please... just please don't let them kill me!"

A heavy silenced followed Martin's intense prayer, and was broken by a sudden knock on the bedroom door. Martin thought it strange, as the knock was not heavy or demanding. Another silence followed. Then, another knock came, and a gentle voice drifted through the door, "Martin? Martin, sweetie. It's Gramma. Please open the door, baby."

The old woman, after hearing the sirens and the screeching of tires, ran out of her neighbor's house and toward the police, screaming that it was her house that they were pointing all their pistols at. Gramma had a feeling that Martin was in there and the he was in a lot of trouble, so she walked stating, "I'm goin' in there, even if you have to shoot me!" She fought, screamed, and yelled, "That's my baby in there!" until the officer in charge told the rest to stand down and let the old woman go in. In a huff, she continued her march to the house and through the open door. She did not see anyone immediately, but knew where to look first. She walked to Martin's bedroom door and tried to turn the knob, but to no avail. Then, she decided to knock, hoping to God that she would get a response and that Martin was alright.

After hearing his grandmother's voice, Martin slowly got off of his knees and carefully walked to the door. He put his ear to it, and could hear nothing but the sound of his grandmother's heavy breathing and a muttering of prayers under her breath. He reached his hand down and slowly, quietly unlocked the door, then he opened it just slightly. He peeked one eye out and saw his Gramma, in tears, standing just to the side.

Gramma looked up and saw Martin gazing at her from inside, then she pushed the door open very gently, so as not to hit the boy's face. She ran in and eagerly, forcefully wrapped her arms around the child who stood looking at the woman pitifully, just as he did when he was much younger. Martin then threw both arms up and around his Gramma, and squeezed her as if it was to be the last time he would have the opportunity to hug the woman who had taken care of him, raised him.

"Are you alright, baby?" Gramma asked the boy after a moment.

"I'm alright," Martin managed to reply with labored breath. "I'm sorry Gramma. I never meant to hurt you, never meant to hurt anybody. I don't know why I did those things. I don't know what's wrong with me. I wish I was good. I wish I could be like everyone else," Martin continued with an angry sob.

"Sshhh," Gramma said as she lifted her hand and rubbed the top of the boy's head. "Listen, baby," she continued. "You may have done some bad things to me, and to others, but there ain't *nothin'* we can do about that *now*. All we got is the present and the future to think about, okay? And, if I can forgive you, and those people can forgive you, and the good Lord can forgive you, you don't have nothin' to worry about, 'cept doin' good things down the road. You hear me, baby? All you need is to forgive yourself," she looked up at Martin whose head was lowered as he listened to his Gramma speak.

"Yes, Gramma," he replied.

"Now, here's what we gonna' do. We got men out there with guns, and they ready to start shootin', so we gonna' slowly walk out that door, and we gonna' give ourselves up to them, okay?"

Martin looked at his grandmother with determination. After a moment's thought, his face contorted in confusion.

"But, Gramma. I can't go to jail. I can still run! I can't be a punk and just give up! I gotta' be a man!"

"A man?! Boy, no man spends his life runnin' from nobody! A man does his best at all times, and does right by those around him. A *man* takes care of his own, and himself! Now, if you run from this problem, the only type of man you'll be is a *dead man!* And I ain't gonna' allow it! I put up with too much, and worked too hard to keep you *here* and away from the sinner's life your mamma' was gonna' give you, to let you go out like that!"

Martin gave his grandmother a hard look. In his mind, he wanted to run, but he could not move, as the passion with which his grandmother spoke, and the ocean of tears streaming down her face, had fought his urge to flee. Then, with eyes yellow with age and red from crying, Gramma looked up at Martin with a strong determination, as if she could use that look to grab ahold of him and keep him locked up and unable to move, unable to run.

The boy then took a breath. He could feel Gramma's arms pulling him nearer. Then, without words, Martin began to walk, Gramma by his side. Slowly, gently, the two sauntered through the front door, Gramma's right arm wrapped tightly around his waist. The two walked closer and closer to the army of officers standing before them. Suddenly, several of them rushed at Martin, one pushed Gramma to the side while another pulled her away. The rest grabbed the boy and threw him to the ground, forced his arms behind his back, and shackled handcuffs around his wrists.

At first, Gramma fought the officer holding her from her grandson, but after realizing that there was nothing more she could do, she loosened her body and cried as the other officers picked Martin up and dragged him to the back seat of one of the many black and white cars that peppered the entire street.

As he sat in the car, Martin could hear nothing but the steady hum of the air conditioner and the exchange of information being sent from one person to the next over the radio. He sat up and looked around, trying to get one last glimpse of his grandmother. He looked out of the window to his left and saw Jackie, Marlene and her daughter standing near the front door of their house. He could see that the two mothers were standing right beside each other sobbing, Marlene in bandages holding Andrea's face close to her thigh, keeping her baby from seeing all that was taking place. Jackie suddenly began walking away, but Martin could not see where she went. He arched his back and extended his neck. He turned and twisted trying to follow the path of his neighbor. Finally, he saw her as she walked up to Gramma, who was seated on the curb, crying with her face buried deep into her hands. Unable to take such a sight, the boy turned away. Then, with his head sunken, tears began to fall, and would not stop until long after he reached the police station.